"You know this is only a pretense!"

Lucy glared at him indignantly as she spoke.

"How prosaic you are," Niccolo replied. "Most women would enjoy pretending to be my wife."

"Nannies can't afford to play such games," she said coolly.

He gave her a languishing look. "Don't they ever fall in love?"

"Only with their own kind."

"How convenient...and what a fallacy!" His tone was gently mocking. "I do not think you know anything about love. It comes suddenly and unexpectedly to the most unlikely couples. I would like to teach you about love, *mia bianca rosa*."

His expression was beguiling, his black eyes soft as velvet. With a supreme effort she threw off the spell of them and retorted coldly, "Aren't your affections already engaged elsewhere, *signor*?"

ELIZABETH ASHTON
is also the author of these
Harlequin Romances

and this
Harlequin Presents

Sicilian Summer

by

ELIZABETH ASHTON

Harlequin Books

TORONTO · LONDON · LOS ANGELES · AMSTERDAM
SYDNEY · HAMBURG · PARIS · STOCKHOLM · ATHENS · TOKYO

Original hardcover edition published in 1980
by Mills & Boon Limited

ISBN 0-373-02401-0

Harlequin edition published May 1981

Printed in U.S.A.

CHAPTER ONE

'*La signorina inglesa.*'

Lucy Loring passed the serving man who had thrown the door open for her and paused on the threshold, unprepared for what she saw. The street side of the Villa di Santa Croce presented an ordinary Italian façade, three stories high, the lower windows tall with flung-back shutters and iron balconies, but the rear of the house looked on to a garden with a view of the sea and the windows of the *salotto* opened on to a wide terrace. The interior of the high-ceilinged room was ornately furnished with settees covered in red plush trimmed with gilt, gilt tables with marble tops, glass cabinets filled with precious objects around its walls, a floor inlaid with mosaics discernible between Persian rugs, and a crystal chandelier hanging from the ceiling. It might be called a villa, but it was more like a palace.

The woman stretched on the wide divan sofa beckoned Lucy forward with a languid hand. She wore a richly embroidered caftan and jewels sparkled at her neck, ears and on her arms. She was handsome in a dark-browed, sultry fashion, and her figure was voluptuous. She was the Contessa di Santa Croce and Lucy's new employer.

There was a second occupant of the room, who had sprung up from his seat beside the Contessa as Lucy was announced, and had taken up a position behind the sofa from where he was appraising the newcomer

out of eyes so dark, pupil and iris seemed as one, surrounded by long black lashes which any girl would
have envied. For a Sicilian he was tall, being above
average height, and his lithe figure had a pantherish
grace. His beautifully shaped mouth was curled in a
sardonic smile as he studied the girl's slight form. Lucy
was as blonde as he was dark, her pale hair drawn back
into a knot in her nape, her grey eyes obscured by sunglasses. She wore a neat linen suit as became her position, in dark blue with a white blouse beneath her
jacket. Her narrow hands nervously gripped her handbag. Though the agency had informed her that the
Conte di Santa Croce was a wealthy man and she could
expect every comfort, she had not been prepared for
such magnificence. There was a touch of Oriental opu-
lence about both the woman and the room, a reminder
that Syracuse had once belonged to the Arabs.

'Come in,' the Contessa said impatiently, 'and take
off those glasses. I wish to look at you.' She spoke
English with an accent.

Lucy advanced to within a few paces of the recum-
bent lady, and obediently removed her sunglasses. The
face thus revealed was classic in its pure outline, straight
nose and rounded chin; her eyes were large and candid
under delicate brows which were much darker than
her pale gold hair. The man behind the sofa drew a
deep breath and the Contessa glanced up at him,
noticed his expression and frowned heavily. She addressed the girl standing before her.

'You are very young, *signorina*.'

'I'm twenty-four, madam, and as the agency will
have told you, I've had six years' experience, and . . .'

The Contessa waved her hand. '*Basta*, I know all

that. Naturally we would not engage you without the highest credentials, but in your photograph you appeared more mature.'

The photograph had been unflattering, for in it Lucy had tried to look suitably severe in order to impress a potential employer. Being in black and white it had not shown her attractive colouring, nor could it catch the play of expression across her mobile face which gave it so much charm. She sensed antagonism in the older woman, though she could not imagine what had aroused it. She had had a hot, tiring journey, culminating in the long drive from the airport, and she was yearning for a drink, though tea she suspected would be undrinkable, if procurable. Nor did the Contessa look the cosy sort of person who would welcome her with that beverage. She glanced upward from the woman to the man standing over her, and met the sensuous gaze of liquid black eyes. Her nerves, already overstrung, responded with a faint thrill. Who was he? she wondered vaguely; not old enough to be the Conte, nor young enough to be the lady's son, but whoever he was he seemed very much at home.

He said something in Italian to the Contessa and the liquid syllables were uttered in a deep musical voice which was as sexy as the rest of him. She replied in English.

'She shall have rest and refreshment in due course, by why concern yourself? She is only the *bambinaia*, but I fear she is quite unsuitable.'

'Surely you will give her a trial?'

'That will not be necessary. One look at her is enough.'

Lucy flushed at this disparagement which she felt was quite unjustified.

'If you wished for an elderly nurse, you should have mentioned it, madam,' she said, 'instead of bringing me all this way for nothing. I was given to understand you wanted someone youthful to look after your daughter, who would be more of a companion for her than the middle-aged person you'd previously employed.'

Annoyance brought a becoming colour into her cheeks, which had been pale with fatigue and caused her eyes to sparkle. Again she caught the young man's glance and his eloquent eyes caused her acute discomfort. There was no doubt about his approval, and she was vaguely aware that his admiration was the source of the Contessa's antagonism. But surely she was not to be condemned because of an Italian wolf's tactless ogling? The look she gave him was scathing, but it only provoked an impudent smile. Lucy had wanted to travel and had jumped at the offer of a job in Sicily. She was looking forward to a sojourn in that country and it was infuriating that her position should be jeopardised by her employer's misjudgment of her, for the last thing she wanted was to be entangled by an amorous male.

'That was my husband's idea,' the Contessa told her acidly. 'A mistaken one in my opinion. A young girl is too irresponsible to take charge of my daughter.' She raised herself to a sitting position. 'You may spend the night here, but tomorrow you must return to England. Your fare will be paid, of course.'

Lucy felt near to tears and bit her lip fiercely as she clutched at her control. To be sent back over all those weary miles without even being given a chance to prove herself, and to arrive at this fascinating island and be banished after only a glimpse of it was a crushing disappointment. And for no good reason, except that she looked younger than the Contessa had anticipated. Wild protests flickered through her mind, but there was something implacable about the attitude of the opulent beauty on the sofa which told her that she would be wasting her breath.

'Whose fare will be paid?'

Lucy turned round as a second man entered the *salotto*. Short and swarthy, he was a typical Sicilian, with a thick thatch of black hair and heavy brows; he was surveying the trio with a suspicious glint in his deep-set eyes.

The Contessa looked disconcerted, then she said quickly:

'The new nannie has arrived. I do not consider she is suitable.'

The older man turned his sombre gaze upon Lucy, surveying her from head to toes, but there was no hint of amorousness in his intent scrutiny. Lucy guessed from his air of authority that he must be the Conte. He was, she judged, about twenty years older than his wife.

'She looks serene . . . and competent,' he remarked.

'Too young,' the Contessa insisted.

'Young companionship is what I want for Carlotta.' He indicated a chair beside him. 'Sit down, *signorina*, I can see you are weary.' He turned to his wife. 'Why have you not given her some refreshment?'

'I do not believe in cosseting . . . servants,' the Contessa said haughtily.

'Then it is not surprising they do not serve you well,'

he retorted, and moving to the wall pressed an old-fashioned bell button.

Lucy sat down gratefully on the chair which he had indicated. It seemed she might be reprieved, but now she was doubtful if she wanted to be. If the Contessa continued to be antagonistic, her position would not be very comfortable. The Conte turned his attention to the younger man.

'Ah, Niccolo, you have honoured us with your presence again.'

'*Si*, Papa. You do not object?'

Papa? But surely he could not be the Contessa's son? Stepson, perhaps. There was animosity in the older man's regard; he was not pleased to find Niccolo alone with his wife. A classic situation? Hippolytus and Phaedra? Lucy felt vaguely disturbed, but their relationships were nothing to do with her. She was an outsider who had come to do a job which now hung in the balance.

'Nicco relieves my boredom,' the Contessa said languidly.

Her husband frowned. 'You could both be better employed,' he said tartly.

'I was only paying my respects to the lady of the house,' Niccolo explained blandly, and spoke rapidly in Italian. The Conte did not respond to whatever he was saying and as a manservant appeared he turned to Lucy.

'Lemonade with ice? *Si*?'

'Thank you, sir, it's just what I'm longing for,' she said gratefully.

The Conte nodded to the man and turned back to Niccolo, intercepting another of those sensuous, speculative glances he was bestowing upon Lucy. A sudden crafty gleam came into his deep set eyes and he shifted his regard to his wife.

'*Bene*, Caterina, I suppose you have prepared accommodation for Signorina ...' he hesitated. 'Lor-ring, was it not?' he rolled the r.

'Yes, *signor*,' Lucy affirmed.

'The nursery suite,' the Contessa said ungraciously. 'But Alfonso ...'

He fixed her with a stern look. 'The young lady stays.'

The servant returned soft-footed with a tall glass on a tray which he offered with deference to Lucy. His master said something in Italian and he again withdrew. The Contessa darted malevolent glances first at her husband and then at the seated girl.

'You are making a mistake,' she insisted.

'Far from it, my dear,' he returned blandly, his eyes mere slits with a cunning gleam between the heavy lids. 'I am being exceedingly far-sighted.' His glance flickered to Niccolo, who was watching Lucy with undisguised interest. She became aware of undercurrents running between the trio of Sicilians, but she was too tired and too relieved to wish to probe further.

'You would like to see your quarters,' her employer suggested. 'And you need rest I am sure. A meal shall be sent up to you, and tomorrow we will discuss your duties. Ah, Giulia!' He addressed a girl in cap and apron who had appeared in the doorway, having been summoned by the man-servant, speaking in her own tongue, apparently giving her some orders.

'You speak Italian, Mees Lor-ring?' he concluded.

'A little,' Lucy admitted.

For the first time he smiled.

'The Sicilian dialect is almost another language, but I dare say you and Giulia can communicate.' He indicated that she should follow the girl and. Lucy stood up. She hesitated, then said:

'Goodnight, madam.' The Contessa inclined her head. Lucy glanced towards Niccolo, but not knowing how to address him, decided to ignore him. She moved towards the door and the waiting Giulia. 'Goodnight, sir.' The smile she gave the Conte was very sweet, for she was grateful to him.

'*Buon riposo,*' he said courteously. Lucy glanced back when she reached the doorway. The Conte had gone to his wife and was, from his expression, reprimanding her. She looked sulky, playing with the necklace at her throat, but Niccolo was watching Lucy with the intentness of a cat at a mousehole. Involuntarily she met that dark, magnetic glance and a shiver ran down her spine. If she stayed, and a faint misgiving hinted that she might be wise to defer to the Contessa's wishes and leave next day, she must avoid that young man like the plague, for instinct warned her he could be just as dangerous.

The nursery suite was at the top of the house, comprising her bedroom, a sitting room and the child's room with a bathroom between them. The sitting room window had french doors and a balcony outside it. She was to learn that all Sicilian houses were prodigal of balconies; this one looked out over the garden towards the sea.

Giulia showed her the rooms with pride and they were comfortably furnished with somewhat old-fashioned pieces, but a television set struck a modern note. Giulia indicated by signs, opening her mouth and pointing to it, that she would bring food. Lucy's cases had been brought up and placed in the bedroom, but before she unpacked, there was something she wanted to see. She stopped Giulia before she could depart, saying:

'*La bambina* ... Carlotta?' For she wanted to be introduced to her charge.

Giulia laid a finger to her lips and opened the other bedroom door. Lucy followed her inside. The small room, which also had access to the bathroom, was furnished with white-painted wood chest and wardrobe; curtains hung at the window, over which the shutters were closed. A nightlight burned beside the pink-draped bed in which the child was lying. Carlotta di Santa Croce was between four and five years old, her limbs still chubby. She had round rosy cheeks, on which the long black eye lashes lay like fans over her closed eyes. Tousled black curls were spread upon the pillow and she was clutching a white woolly dog. A lovely, healthy child, Lucy saw with relief, and though being a Sicilian she no doubt had her share of hot temper she did not look sulky or unmanageable. Lucy caught the tender smile of Giulia's lips and recalled that Sicilians were supposed to be devoted to children. It was possible young Carlotta was terribly spoiled.

She followed Giulia back into the sitting room, leaving the door slightly ajar; the child seemed so solitary at the top of that huge house. Giulia nodded her approval.

Left alone, Lucy explored her territory. Her bedroom and the sitting room looked out at the back of

the house, while Carlotta's was to the side. There was
a small alcove next to the bathroom containing an electric kettle and a cupboard with tins of biscuits and
coffee essence—English brands, she noticed with a
smile She unpacked her cases, putting her somewhat
meagre collection of dresses in the wardrobe and her
underwear in the drawers. She had brought plain white
linen dresses and several overalls as being suitable for
the climate and her duties. She had included a pair of
slacks and several tops to wear on her off days, when
she hoped to be able to explore the island.

After Giulia had brought her a meal—an omelette,
cheese and fruit—and removed the tray, she changed
into her dressing gown, a glamorous pale blue negligee,
her one extravagance, and with her hair loose about
her shoulders went out on to the balcony for a final
survey of her surroundings before going to bed. The
villa was situated on the outskirts of the town, which
was on her right, throwing a ruddy glow into the sky,
and the darkened sea was spangled with the lights of
vessels. Syracuse was, as she knew, the ancient capital
of Sicily in the days of the Greeks and Romans. It had
been a centre of art and learning, besides being a
fortress. The tyrant Dionysius had made Ortygia, the
peninsula off the coast, almost impregnable against
Sicily's most virulent enemy, Carthage. Its Greek
theatre had been famous throughout the Attic world;
the poet Aeschylus had presented some of his tragedies
there. But Syracuse fell to invaders in the end, and
after the Arab conquest the capital was moved to
Palermo.

A movement on the terrace below her caused Lucy
to look down. Foreshortened by the distance was a

male figure, which from its attitude appeared to be gazing upward. The spilled light from an open window shone on black hair and a white jacket, illuminated also Lucy's loosened locks, turning them to a cascade of silver-gilt, amid which her face showed a luminous oval. The thin stuff of her wrap clung to her shoulders and the slight swell of her breasts. The night breeze stirred the palms and cypresses in the garden, releasing a wave of exotic scents from the flowering shrubs. The rustle of leaves was echoed in the man's low appreciative whistle. Lucy turned quickly and re-entered her room. The last thing she wanted was to play Juliet to the predatory Romeo on the terrace. She was vaguely disturbed and angry that he had broken the fragrant calm of the night, but when at length she fell asleep, it was his dark face which haunted her dreams.

Lucy was awakened by Carlotta bouncing on her bed. Evidently Giulia had attended to her, for she was fully dressed in a white embroidered frock, white socks and patent shoes. Later Lucy discovered that Giulia had been detailed to wait upon herself and her charge.

'*Buon giorno,*' the child said. 'You my new *bambinaia*?' Carlotta was bi-lingual, as her previous nurse had been English.

'Yes.' Lucy rubbed the sleep out of her eyes. The Conte had said in the preliminary correspondence that he wished his daughter to become proficient in English and besides always speaking it together he hoped she would give the child some lessons. Though strictly speaking she was not a governess, Lucy had agreed, for the salary he offered was munificent.

'I hope you and I are going to be good friends,' she went on.

Carlotta extended a chubby hand and touched her hair.

'Pretty.'

'I'm glad you think so.'

'Other *bambinaia brutta*,' the child informed her. '*Brutta e vecchia*.'

'Speak English, please,' Lucy said automatically, while she digested this description of her predecessor. The Conte had said he wanted someone young to take charge of his daughter, but his wife would have preferred the mixture as before. She wondered why the middle-aged nannie had left.

'She not like Sicily,' Carlotta answered her thought. 'You like it?'

'I'm sure I shall.'

'Zio Nicco say good riddance when she go,' Carlotta went on pronouncing the two unfamiliar words carefully. 'What that mean, *bambinaia*?'

'That he didn't like her,' Lucy suggested, thinking Zio Nicco should be more careful what he said in his niece's hearing, if she were his niece. 'Does he live here?' she added anxiously. To be liked by Niccolo might be dangerous.

Carlotta shook her curly head. 'No, he have own place. *Mia mamma* like him very, very much. *Mio papa* ...' She shrugged her shoulders expressively.

'Oh!' Lucy reflected that Carlotta's unconsciously indiscreet tongue could be a menace. 'But your *papa* ought to love his son.'

'Zio Nicco not his son,' Carlotta declared, thereby mystifying her nannie. The child called him uncle, but that was probably a courtesy title as used by most children to describe male friends of the family. But it was not her place to use Carlotta to unravel the Santa Croce relationships which doubtless she would learn in time.

'I must get dressed,' she said briskly, throwing back the bed clothes, and Carlotta studied her nylon nightdress with interest.

'Pretty,' she said again, and smiled beatifically. 'Pretty lady, pretty clothes.'

'Thank you, but . . .'

Giulia appeared and addressed the child in a flood of Italian. To Lucy she said something in which she caught the word '*bagno.*' So she was expected to have a bath, and nothing would please her more. She sprang out of bed, snatched up her clothes and made for the bathroom where she found Giulia had run her bath and liberally scented it with bath essence. While she soaked away the lingering fatigue of the journey, Lucy wondered why she was given such special treatment; she had not expected the services of a ladies' maid. Later on the Conte explained.

He sent for her after breakfast, interviewing her in the room which was obviously his private sanctum, as it was austerely furnished in dark leather and contained an imposing desk. Her work was mainly to supervise Giulia, who would do all the domestic chores for both of them and attend to Carlotta's toilet, while Lucy was to be a companion to his daughter, teaching her English. She was a bright little thing, he said fondly, and quite old enough to do simple lessons in other subjects if Mees Lor-ring would be so obliging. They could walk in the garden, but . . . Here he paused and seemed to be considering what to say.

'Can I take her to the beach?' Lucy enquired, knowing how children loved to play in the sand, and there must be plenty of that around since Syracuse was a seaport.

'That is what I am coming to,' Alfonso di Santa Croce frowned heavily. 'I would like her to see the ancient monuments which are part of her heritage, as well as being educational, but you must never, never leave the house unescorted. There will be trusted servants to accompany you everywhere.' He smiled ruefully. 'A bodyguard.'

Startled, Lucy stared at him.

'Is that really necessary?'

'Yes. I am, Mees Lor-ring, a very rich man. You must know from recent cases in the papers that because of that my daughter is at risk ... even here in Sicily. You must never leave her alone and always have protection when you go out.'

'I see.' Lucy began to understand why the *brutta* and *vecchia* lady had left. 'It is a great responsibility, *signore*.'

He looked at her keenly.

'Are you afraid to assume it?'

Lucy reflected that if this aspect of her job had been put to her in London, she might have hesitated, but since she was actually there it seemed cowardly to throw in her hand. Moreover, she was eager to see something of the country.

'Well, I ...'

'Mind you, the risk is minimal,' her employer went on. 'This is not Rome and my people are very loyal to me, but I am taking no chances and neither must you.'

'I understand,' she said quietly. 'You can rely on me.'

It seemed she would earn her generous salary; the

risk might be small, but it would always be there.

'Good.' A smile lightened the Conte's heavy features. 'You shall have one day a week to yourself to go where you please. On those occasions Giulia and Franco—he is my most trustworthy servant—will be in charge. You can be free as air.'

She thanked him, thinking how she would look forward to those days of liberty.

'My wife,' the Conte continued, his face setting in stern lines, 'takes little interest in the child. She will not interfere with any routine you care to devise. She wanted a son, you understand, but we have not been so blessed, though I still hope.' He relapsed into brooding silence, and Lucy surmised that all was not as it should be between husband and wife. Presently he roused himself to say: 'I myself visit my child once a day when I am at home, usually in the mornings when you will be doing lessons.'

Poor Carlotta, Lucy thought, how dependent she must have been on the former nannie, with no real family life—a neglectful mother and a busy father.

'She has no little friends? No visitors?' she asked.

'Oh yes, we have friends who bring their little ones from time to time. You will be advised when to expect them. And there is Signor Martelli.' He looked at her directly with a curious glint in his eyes. 'He is very fond of the child. You have already met him.'

'Zio Nicco?' She smiled. 'Carlotta spoke of him.' She hesitated. 'Is he to be encouraged?'

This time the Conte's smile was very wry.

'In every way,' he told her.

'Oh, but he may be a disturbing influence.' Lucy

was appalled by the thought of Romeo having free
access to the nursery.

'We must chance that.' The look he gave her was
enigmatical. 'I prefer him in the nursery rather than
the *salotto*.'

So he was not blind to what was going on between
his wife and the young man. Lucy moved uneasily. If
she were to be enlisted as a counter-attraction she did
not relish the situation at all.

'Who is he?' she asked bluntly. 'Carlotta said he was
not your son.'

The Conte sighed. 'As much a son as I seem likely to
have. I have been married before, but my first wife
died young. She had been left a widow with an infant
son and a great estate which she was incapable of managing. It seemed a most suitable alliance.' His voice
trailed away as he gazed unseeingly before him, and
Lucy remembered that arranged marriages were still
in force among many Italian families, especially Sicilians. A rich young widow would be considered a catch
even if she did have a child.

The Conte recalled himself from his brooding, and
he had something to brood about. Two wives and still
no son to inherit his vast wealth.

'I brought Nicco up as my own child,' he said
harshly. 'If I have no son of my own, I may make him
my heir, if he behaves himself, but he has always been
an insubordinate young cub. Unfortunately when he
came of age he acquired part of his mother's estate, so
I have no control over him ...' He broke off. 'All this
has nothing to do with you, *signorina*, but it is as well
you should understand the situation. He is fond of
Carlotta and she of him. If I could obtain a dispensa-

tion, they might wed eventually.' Again the brooding
look, while Lucy sought to recall the Table of Affinity.
Deceased wife's son—no blood relation of course to
Carlotta, but a long time to wait until the child was
marriageable. No blood relation either to the present
wife, however it was regarded by the Church of Rome.

One thing stuck out a mile; these purse-proud Sicilians would have no use whatever for an alliance with
an English nonentity. Why ever should she think of
that? Merely as a useful warning that if the fascinating
Niccolo Martelli did make advances his intentions
would be strictly dishonourable.

She glanced apprehensively at the man in front of
her. He was as cynical and unscrupulous as he was
proud. If he saw in her a means to divert his stepson's
fancy from his wife, he would not hesitate to promote
their intimacy without caring in the least how devastating the consequences might be to herself.

To the devil with the lot of them! she thought
angrily; she was only concerned with making life hap-
pier for the poor little rich girl upstairs. But fore-
warned was forearmed, and if Niccolo came prowling
round her nursery, he would be shown very definitely
that only Carlotta welcomed him. As for the threat
which hung over the child, she would in time come
to live with it. People lived quite happily on the slopes
of Mount Etna, without heeding the mountain's subterranean grumblings.

The Conte emerged from his sombre thoughts, and
gave her a charming smile. He could be attractive
too, she thought, when he chose.

'I have been frank with you, Mees Lor-ring, and I
am sure you will respect my confidence,' he declared.

'You are exactly what I want for Carlotta, young and bright, and I am sure you will not be too strict. It is not discipline that she needs, but affection. I hope my precautions have not frightened you and you will stay and do your best for her?'

'Oh, yes, I'll stay.' Lucy burned her boats. 'I love Carlotta already, and I'll do my very best to make her happy.'

But not to provide a diversion for Signor Niccolo Martelli. That he could find elsewhere.

CHAPTER TWO

LUCY's days soon fell into an orderly routine. The weather became hotter as spring passed into summer, so she rose early, bathed or showered and assisted Giulia to wash and dress Carlotta. After a continental breakfast of fresh rolls, butter, preserves and coffee they would go out into the garden while it was still cool. The extensive grounds to the rear of the villa were enclosed by very high walls with spikes on top of them, ensuring privacy and security. Even so, Lucy was always conscious of Franco or some other guardian hovering in the distance. The gardens were for the most part formally laid out, neat flower beds interspersed with flowering shrubs, with the occasional marble statue. But there was one strip of lawn under the wall where they could play games. A miniature putting green had been set out and there was a swing and a see-saw, but what Carlotta enjoyed most was hitting a tennis ball against the wall, though she most often than not missed its bounce, using the small raquet specially made for her.

They would return for lessons, speaking and writing English, varied with drawing or modelling with Plasticine. Lucy tried to interest the child in the history of her country and the classic world that had done so much to mould it. She was not a qualified teacher, her diplomas were for child care, but she had the gift of being able to hold her pupil's attention.

Lunch was brought to them and they ate most of

their meals on the wide balcony outside their window, over which a sun blind was drawn to give them shade. Then followed the siesta during the heat of the early afternoon. After tea, Carlotta did her piano practice, and Lucy would read or tell her stories, for which the child was avid, especially fairy-tales.

The Conte visited them most mornings, sometimes taking coffee with them. He conversed with his daughter as if she were an adult, but she looked forward to his coming, since he usually brought her a new toy or a book. The Contessa only came when she had visitors who wanted to dump their children in the nursery while they gossiped with their hostess. This oc-cured once or twice a week and the little girls and boys were almost painfully well-behaved. Only rarely did the Sicilian tempers flare up, usually over a dispute as to who should play with what, for Carlotta did oc-casionally become possessive over her toys. Then Lucy glimpsed a depth of volcanic passion which rather shocked her. When provoked, Carlotta's 'I hate you, you horrid thing, I want to kill you,' was uttered with a ferocity that was spine chilling. Nor did she stop at words, and Lucy would have to separate two furious small combatants before they seriously damaged each other. They would sulk for the remainder of the visit, but when they met again, all had been forgotten.

Sundays were Lucy's days off. Carlotta went to church with her parents and had lunch with them in the im-posing *sala di pranzo*. The repressions of the day would end in a display of temper and tears, when Lucy re-turned in the evening. How she longed to dress her charge in shorts and tee-shirt instead of her over long dresses and take her to play on the beach, dig in the sand and paddle—but she knew such informality would never be allowed.

The routine was further varied by the tutor who came once a week to give piano lessons, and dancing classes held in the small ballroom belonging to the villa to which the friends' children were brought. Occasionally they went under heavy escort to a riding school, where Carlotta jogged round under cover upon a fat pony. Lucy, who could ride herself, thought regretfully of canters over greensward which it seemed would always be denied her charge.

It was over two weeks before Lucy again saw Niccolo Martelli. He breezed in one morning when they were finishing breakfast. Lucy heard the door open and thought it was Giulia, until Carlotta gave an ecstatic squeal, tumbled off her chair and rushed back through the window.

'Zio ... Zio Nicco!'

He came out on to the balcony with the little girl riding on his shoulders. He had been riding himself, for he was wearing very well cut breeches and polished boots with a thin pullover. Lucy had forgotten how good-looking he was and the equestrian outfit became him. He looked elegant and debonair.

'*Buon giorno, signorina,*' he greeted her. 'Is there perhaps a cup of coffee left in that pot? I am thirsty after my morning gallop.'

'I think so. I'll rinse out a cup.' Lucy rose to her feet.

'*Signorina,* do not discommode yourself. This bad girl will do it.' He put Carlotta on her feet. 'Infant, be useful as well as ornamental.'

'What's that?' Carlotta demanded.

'What every woman should aspire to be. Run along,

I am waiting with my tongue hanging out.'

'It isn't!' Carlotta stared at his mouth.

'I assure you it will be if you don't hurry.'

Carlotta disappeared with the cup making for the bathroom. Niccolo sat down on her vacated chair. Lucy found the narrow confines of the balcony brought him too near for comfort; he exuded masculine vigour and charisma, which affected her nerves, even while she despised herself for such schoolgirlish weakness. The sloe-black eyes regarded her quizzically under his level brows.

'Well, how are you enjoying the luxurious living at the Villa Santa Croce?' he enquired. '*Mio papa* does not stint you, I am sure, and you look blooming.'

'Everything is wonderful.' But she sighed.

'Something is missing?'

'Freedom.'

Carlotta returned with the clean cup and Lucy poured the coffee, wondering what had made her say such a thing and to a complete stranger. It was what she missed, being able to come and go, except upon her days off, and more for her charge's sake than her own. She would like to take Carlotta out shopping, walking, without the surveillance of a bodyguard, which she knew was impossible.

'Wealth and privilege have their drawbacks,' Niccolo remarked as he sipped his coffee.

'So it seems ... in this country.'

Carlotta interrupted. 'Where you been, Zio? Long time no see.'

'On my estates, sugar, first Calabria to see how the sheep were doing, then Valpena to look at the vines.'

'Valpena?' Carlotta looked at him eagerly. 'That's

on Etna. You promised to show me the volcano ... all flames.'

'Etna isn't always erupting,' Nicco explained. 'I shall have to try to arrange a special show for you when you come.'

'Do people actually live on its slopes?' Lucy asked, her interest caught.

'Certainly they do. The soil is particularly fertile. I have a house there and the city of Catania is situated right underneath it. Nowadays we usually know when the mountain is about to vomit and can get out of the way in time.'

'But don't you lose everything?'

'That is a matter of luck – the way the lava flows. So far Valpena has always escaped. It is a charming place, *signorina*, which lacks only one thing.'

'Safety, I should imagine,' Lucy said drily.

'Bah, who cares for that?' He snapped his fingers. 'To live dangerously gives a spice to life. Its lack is a mistress.'

He gave her a sidelong look, which Lucy refused to meet.

'Surely you can easily remedy that,' she said stolidly.

He shook his head mournfully, though his eyes were brimful of mischief.

'Alas, not many girls want to live on the slopes of Etna, even with myself as an inducement. They have no spirit of adventure, unlike you, *signorina*, who must have plenty to come to Syracuse.'

'Which is satisfied for the present,' she returned, wondering what he was getting at. Valpena was nothing to do with her.

Carlotta chipped in. 'When I big lady, you marry

me, Zio. I like to live there.'

'It is a thought,' Niccolo agreed, 'but I should have to exist in uncomfortable celibacy for twelve to fourteen years, at the end of which time you might have changed your mind.'

'*No*,' Carlotta declared emphatically. 'I love you, Zio Nicco.' She nuzzled against him like a pet puppy.

'Such adoration is most gratifying, but I am afraid you will feel differently when you are grown up,' Nicco sighed.

Lucy rose to her feet. 'I'm sorry, but lesson time will have to curtail your love scene. I'm not sure if my duties include those of chaperone, but they do entail regular hours.'

'What is chaperone?' Carlotta demanded.

'A sort of dragon,' Nicco told her, 'and I see you have one here now. I have been away for ... what is it? Two whole weeks, and when at last I am reunited with my lady love, she would separate us with the three Rs.'

'Are you really engaged to Carlotta?' Lucy asked, remembering what the Conte had said. 'Isn't she a bit young for you?'

'I will be no older when she is marriageable than the Conte was when he married Carlotta's *mama*,' Niccolo drawled. 'But you are all for romantic marriages in your country, are you not, *signorina*, though judging by the divorce rate they do not work out very well. In Sicily we have no divorce.'

'But I thought the Italian government ...'

'I said in Sicily. Here we obey our church implicitly. But I trespass on your time.' He pushed Carlotta away and stood up. 'Thank you for the coffee, and I warn you you will be seeing a great deal of me now I am back.'

'You mean Carlotta will.' Lucy hesitated. His affection for the child had touched her, it seemed to be perfectly genuine. She wondered if she dared enlist his aid on the little girl's behalf.

'Couldn't you . . .' she began, and paused.

'Could I . . . what?'

'Suggest to her parents she should go out more, see something of the country, and be allowed to play on the beach, ride in the country.'

'In fact make her into a hoyden as no doubt you were.' He drew himself up haughtily. 'My future wife has to be trained to be a lady.'

Lucy turned away, with difficulty restraining her anger at the implied rebuke. Perhaps it was better for Carlotta to be brought up in her country's rigid tradition, but she could not believe it would make her happy. The child was bursting with sheer animal spirits which needed a physical outlet. She was surprised to hear Niccolo say behind her, without the derisory note in his voice:

'I have not much hope of influencing the Conte's views, and I know he is old-fashioned, and you know Carlotta has to be protected, but I will help you if I can.'

She turned back to him, her face aglow. 'Thank you so much! It seems she never goes beyond the house and grounds except to riding school, and as she has told you, she hasn't even seen Etna.'

Carlotta added her plea to hers. 'Want to see fire mountain. Want see lots, lots of things. I hate the old garden!'

Niccolo smiled down into her eager face.

'I must see what can be arranged,' he promised.

Upon reflection, Lucy regretted her appeal to him, for Carlotta was not his business; he was not even a blood relation. If he did appeal to the Conte on her behalf, it was unlikely his words would have any effect, and if they did, she would feel under an obligation to him, which was not a situation she appreciated, even on Carlotta's account. She feared he might report what she had said to the Contessa, who would regard it as an indication of her irresponsibility. In the event what did occur was so bizarre she would never have credited it in her wildest imaginings.

Two days later they had settled down to what they termed English conversation—which was a process of question and answer, Carlotta being the questioner; she was insatiably curious about life in England and how little English girls spent their time—when Giulia brought a message. The Contessa wished to see Mees in the *salotto—pronto, pronto!* Giulia baulked at pronouncing Lucy's name and always referred to her as Mees.

Lucy received the summons with a sinking heart. Niccolo must have reported her complaint in the wrong quarter as she had feared, and she was going to be reprimanded for exceeding her duties. She glanced at Carlotta and Giulia indicated that she would stay with the child.

'Go *presto*,' she said, for she was picking up some English words. 'Madonna no like to wait.'

Lucy went.

In the *salotto*, which she had not entered since the day of her arrival, she found not only the Contessa but her husband as well. Caterina was looking furious and Lucy's heart sank, but the Conte was all smiles.

'Ah, Mees Lor-ring,' he greeted her amiably. 'I have been told you consider Carlotta is too confined to the house and grounds and she should participate in outdoor activities. About that I have reservations, but you also said it would assist her education if she saw more of her own country and its historic monuments.'

'I'm afraid I rather forgot my place,' Lucy apologised. 'I've no right to question the way in which you bring up your daughter.'

Here his wife interrupted with a flood of Italian, evidently endorsing Lucy's words. The Conte heard her out politely, but he did not seem impressed. When she had finished, he said calmly to Lucy:

'My wife clings to the old conventions, and is naturally concerned for our daughter's safety, but I am entirely in agreement with what you say, Mees. Carlotta will have to live in a very different world from the one you and your parents knew, my dear Caterina, and even at her tender age should see more of what goes on around her. Also she will learn to appreciate her country's great past if she sees the monuments that commemorate it.'

'Quite unnecessary,' the Contessa said in English. 'She will go to a convent school in due course and thence, I hope, into the arms of a suitable husband whom we shall select for her.'

The Conte smiled wryly. 'Convent schools are not what they used to be,' he remarked, 'and with women nowadays even going into politics, Carlotta's development must not be stunted, as yours was, my dear. Had you been encouraged to take a greater interest in intel-

lectual pursuits, you might not need to relieve your
boredom with more questionable amusements.'

The Conte's deep-set eyes were filled with malice, as
his wife shot him a glance of pure hatred.

'If you did not neglect me ...' she began, but he
interrupted her with a wave of his hand.

'We were discussing Carlotta,' he reminded her. He
turned to Lucy. 'The seclusion in which my daughter is
kept is, as you know, for her own safety, but I have
thought of a way in which you can go about without
undue risk. Signor Martelli has kindly offered to be
your escort ...'

'I refuse to allow it!' Caterina burst in, while Lucy
was filled with consternation. When she had made
her plea to Niccolo for her charge's greater freedom,
she had no inkling that he would take a personal interest in achieving it. She had no wish to be brought into
greater intimacy with him, for her instinct warned her
that a closer contact with him could do her no good,
and would very much annoy the Contessa, as the fury
on her handsome face plainly indicated.

'I give the orders in this house,' her husband told
her, 'and if Nicco wishes to oblige me, why should you
object?'

The Contessa made a visible effort to contain her
rage and chagrin.

'It is not a suitable arrangement,' she said loftily.
'Niccolo is a young man connected with the nobility,
while Mees Lor-ring ...'

'Is a young lady of great good sense,' the Conte
interrupted suavely. 'She will, I am sure, not get ideas
above her station.' He smiled at Lucy kindly.

'It is very kind of Signor Martelli to offer,' Lucy

told him guardedly, 'but I'm sure he'll find such expeditions tedious.'

The Conte's smile became cunning. 'I do not think so,' he said significantly, and the Contessa exclaimed indignantly:

'Think of the girl's reputation!'

'You should be more concerned with your own,' her husband retorted coldly. 'Your objections, my dear Caterina, are too revealing.'

His wife flushed a dark red and picked at her skirt with restless fingers. She was obviously seething with suppressed emotions which she dared not express in her husband's presence.

Lucy said quietly:

'*Signor*, if the Contessa so dislikes the arrangement, I would much prefer you would think no more about it.'

'I put Carlotta's welfare before my wife's prejudices,' he told her. 'And since you advocated the innovation it does not become you to protest.'

Lucy was silent, but she was uneasily aware that it was not Carlotta's education that was primarily motivating her father. The Conte was a very subtle man and his wife's conduct had deeply incensed him. Niccolo's offer had given him a chance to wound his wife, for he knew from his own experience how painful were the pangs of jealousy. Lucy was only a pawn in his game of tit for tat and short of resigning her position, which she did not want to do, she had no option but to fall in with his scheming. What Niccolo expected to gain by his offer was not apparent, she did not flatter herself it could be more than a passing interest in her company and any attempt at seduction would be sternly nipped in the bud. She decided he would soon grow tired of escorting his courtesy niece and her governess about the countryside, especially if she was not forthcoming. Possibly he was attracted by a new face, and she had nothing but contempt for a man who could so easily divert his attentions, as it was perfectly obvious that he was involved with the elder woman and that was what had roused the Conte's desire for vengeance.

Meanwhile her official employer, for Caterina was that, was very close to becoming a bitter enemy, which was disquieting. If only she had had the good sense to hold her tongue in Nicollo's presence—but she had never dreamed that he would take it upon himself to be the instrument by which Carlotta's freedom was to be obtained. Moreover, it was only a very limited freedom at that and hardly worth the controversy. Being dragged round temples and museums was not what she really wanted for her charge, but there was one compensation; she would see all the places she wanted to visit herself and with no effort on her part.

'*Bene*, that is all settled, then,' the Conte said with an air of finality, ignoring his wife's murderous expression. 'I will let you know, my dear Mees, what Signor Martelli's arrangements are in due course. You may go now.'

He had the complacent air of a man who had completed a satisfactory transaction.

Dismissed, Lucy inclined her head towards the enraged Contessa and moved towards the door at the opposite end of the long room. To her surprise, the Conte walked beside her and opened it for her with a flourish. A thought struck her.

'The bodyguard will accompany us, I suppose?'

He shook his head.

'I do not think that will be necessary. You will in-struct Carlotta to address Signor Martelli as Papa on these outings, and he will refer to you as his wife. You will appear to be just an inconspicuous little family party.'

Lucy, half out of the door, turned and stared at him aghast.

'*Signore* . . .' she started to protest.

'You must see that would be a very good arrange-ment,' he cut her short. 'Niccolo has been out of the country for some time, his domestic affairs are not common knowledge and the appearance of a wife and child will surprise nobody, though of course his im-mediate family know better. It is my enemies of the underworld that are to be deceived, and they will ac-cept you for what you appear to be.'

'*Signore*, I can't consent to such a cloak and dagger proceeding,' Lucy began, her consternation growing.

'Why not? Are not cloaks and daggers what you ex-pect of Sicilianos? In a country where vendettas are still a way of life and the Mafia is notorious we have to resort to such deceptions to protect our own.'

He glanced back at his wife, who was glowering at them from her sofa with such menace that Lucy was sure it was not only his child he sought to protect with such subterfuges. Jealousy, vindictiveness and cunning were concealed beneath his suave amiability. But to pose as Niccolo's wife was too much to ask of her, but before she could make further protests he gently pushed her through the door and closed it behind her. Lucy heard the Contessa's voice raised in vituperation through the panels of the door, and the Conte's cold cutting replies, but as they spoke in Italian she could not catch the actual words.

Lucy hurried back to her own domain determined to refuse to accept the unwelcome role he sought to thrust upon her. She was disconcerted when upon opening her sitting room door she found Niccolo waiting for her with confident complacency. She had already decided that the Conte's outrageous suggestion was less to deceive possible kidnappers than to annoy his wife, but it would put her in an impossible position with regard to the man in front of her. With the knowledge that he was party to his stepfather's impossible proposal, sudden anger shook her, causing her cheeks to glow and her eyes to sparkle irefully.

Niccolo shoved Carlotta off his knee and rose to greet her, surveying her with lazy insolence.

'Is is triumph which causes your eyes to shine?' he asked. '*Il maestro* has capitulated, has he not, and I have won your freedom for you.'

'On the contrary,' she retorted, restraining her fury with difficulty, 'you've gone and put your foot in it good and proper!'

The level black eyebrows rose at her tone. Niccolo was looking exceedingly handsome, wearing the riding gear which set off his lithe elegant figure to advantage. In spite of her indignation, Lucy felt a stir of her senses as she met the sensuous regard of his black eyes.

'I did what you asked,' he said reproachfully. 'Papa sees your point. He is all for it, and this very afternoon I propose to take you to see our Greek and Roman amphitheatres. Is not that what you wish?'

She looked down, unable to meet the sudden gleam

in his eyes, which betrayed that he knew the terms upon which the concession was gained.

'I'm grateful for your efforts,' she said in a tone which expressed no gratitude whatever. 'But I don't like the proposed conditions.'

Niccolo gave a low laugh and turned to the expectant Carlotta.

'Little one, would you not like to be my little girl and Mees to be your *mamma*? Don't you think it would be a delightful arrangement?'

Carlotta regarded him solemnly. 'I like you to be my *papa* ver' much, but Mees cannot be my *mamma*. She not make me in her tummy.'

This unexpected revelation that Carlotta knew the facts of life convulsed Niccolo and covered Lucy with confusion.

'You can pretend she did,' Niccolo suggested, giving Lucy a sidelong look.

Carlotta considered this idea.

'Like a fairy-tale?' she asked.

'Just like a fairy-tale, and we all three will be happy ever after.'

'You're optimistic,' Lucy told him, recovering herself. 'It's most impracticable. To start with, no one with eyes to see would ever believe I was Carlotta's mother.'

'They would if I was Papa,' Niccolo corrected her. 'It is a biological fact that the dark blood predominates.'

The look he gave her was so audacious that Lucy blushed faintly. He noticed it with delight.

'A girl who can still blush!' he exclaimed.

'The situation is enough to make any respectable girl blush,' she retorted hotly, 'really, *signore*, I *cannot* go around the country posing as your wife.'

'Why not? It is not as though you are expected to sleep with me,' he said bluntly, hoping to provoke another blush, and he was not disappointed. 'It is to protect Carlotta,' he pointed out.

'But will it? You too are a wealthy man, aren't you?'

His eyes narrowed suspiciously. 'I do not possess enough to tempt kidnappers ... or gold-diggers. I could not raise millions of lire in ransom money.'

Lucy remembered Carlotta and threw him a warning glance, but the child had not taken in the significance of his words, though Lucy herself had not missed the reference to gold-diggers—a most unnecessary caution if it were meant for herself. What Carlotta had realised was that the promised expedition had been jeopardised, and she cried out anxiously:

'Me want go. You horrid to tell Zio we can't!' She stamped an imperious foot. 'Zio, make Mees be my *mamma!*'

Niccolo laughed. 'Surely you cannot resist that command? By the way, what do I call you? Naturally I must use your first name.'

'It's Lucy,' she said shortly.

'How appropriate! The patron saint of Syracuse is Santa Lucia.' The elequent black eyes caressed her. 'Lucee ... it suits you, but I hope you are not too saint-like.'

'I try to be,' she retorted primly, 'but I won't ...'

'Mees—I mean Mamma,' Carlotta broke in pleadingly, 'we go, yes, yes, please?'

The child's eyes were equally eloquent and Lucy could not resist their appeal.

'Well, perhaps this once ...' she began.

'And after this once you will find how delightful the experience is, for I will take great care of you, *mia moglie*, so you will want to go again and yet again,' Niccolo said confidently.

'We'll see about that,' Lucy returned coolly, not recognising the word he had used, which meant wife. 'But suppose we meet friends of yours? They would know.'

'We will deal with that eventually if it arises,' he told her. 'To them of course you would be Carlotta's nannie, but I have not a great many acquaintances here and it would be bad luck if we encounter any.'

'I tell all you my *mamma*,' Carlotta declared helpfully.

Niccolo caressed her black curls.

'Don't overdo it, infant,' he drawled. 'it is quite enough if the rank and file assume we are a family.'

Which remark was above Carlotta's head.

He said he would call for them after siesta time when the midday heat was cooling, and in spite of her qualms Lucy's spirits rose at the prospect of the expedition, for so far her explorations on her Sundays off had not taken her far afield. Franco, he told them would let them out by a side gate at the end of the garden, which he informed them with a grin was the entry the servants used when returning from their nocturnal assignments. He would be waiting for them there with his car parked at a distance.

'Not my usual sports car,' he said regretfully, 'that would be too conspicuous, but an ordinary Fiat. *Madonna mia*, infant, the sacrifices I make for you!'

A regret Lucy did not share; she thought they would be much safer in an ordinary Fiat.

'Clothes,' he went on. 'You must wear what the tourists do. You possess trousers, Lucy?' She started as he used her name, but she must accept that, and she nodded briefly.

'I do not like the garments,' he declared with his eyes on her slim ankles, 'so unfeminine, but necessary for our purpose. Now, Carlotta.'

'Shorts and a shirt, but she doesn't possess them,' Lucy told him.

'Then Giulia must procure some.'

Giulia was summoned, and the three of them enjoyed themselves measuring the child for shorts, shirt and sandals. Lucy held aloof watching them a little scornfully, finding the charade a little absurd until it occurred to her that the cloak and dagger technique was part of their Sicilian heritage. Intrigue was in their blood, part of their passionate, vengeful natures. She knew very well the present masquerade was not designed wholly for Carlotta's protection, for as such there were too many holes in it, but to serve the Conte's subtle purposes. By encouraging intimacy between Lucy and his stepson he hoped to break his association with his wife. Caterina di Santa Croce was also Sicilian, and she could hardly be expected to take his manoeuvring without reprisals. Recalling her dark vindictive face, Lucy felt a cold shiver down her spine. In what dark depths had she allowed herself to become involved?

CHAPTER THREE

Lucy stood on the stage of the vast Greco-Roman amphitheatre gazing in wonderment up at the semi-circle of stone seats which could accommodate ten thousand spectators. Niccolo and Carlotta stood beside her, and the little girl, feeling overawed, clung to her hand. They had already explored the *Anatonia del Paradiso*, the exotic gardens among the grey stone quarries, and visited the ropemakers' grotto and the cave to which the *Orecchio di Dionigi* gave access. That extraordinary cleft in the rock was shaped like a human ear, but the legend that Dionysius, tyrant of Syracuse, had used its peculiar acoustic properties to eavesdrop on the occupants of the Latomia, Niccolo dismissed as a myth. Carlotta was puzzled by the huge 'ear'. '*Dionigi* must have had a *molto grande* head,' she remarked, 'and where is the other ear?'

She had been self-conscious at first in her boyish garb, but seeing so many other children similarly clad, she began to enjoy the freedom of movement her shorts allowed.

Contrarily Lucy missed Franco's protective presence, which she had formerly resented, and had anxiously surveyed every male Siciliano in sight, but the crowd was mainly composed of foreign tourists, and she realised that Niccolo had been right when he had said that they would be quite inconspicuous among them. The only people who gave them a second glance were youths and girls, the former being attracted by Lucy's pensive beauty and the latter by Niccolo's good looks. He, she noticed returned their interest if the women were pretty, and she wondered, if he had been alone, if he would have responded to the open invitation so many of them blatantly offered.

Carlotta soon lost her awe of her surroundings. Noticing several children were climbing valiantly up the broken stairways that bisected the seating, she let go of Lucy's hand and ran forward, crying; 'Me want to climb top!'

'Should she ...' Lucy began doubtfully, looking at Niccolo.

'She will be all right. I can soon catch up with her if she gets into difficulties. Let her be independent for once.'

There were stepped gangways between the rows of seats and it was up one of these that Carlotta was toiling in the wake of two older children, whom she was eager to overtake. Lucy feared the heat and exertion might be too much for her, and then chided herself for being over-protective. She had wanted freedom for Carlotta, and now she was experiencing it, though not quite in the way Lucy had envisaged.

As she watched the small figure gamely scrambling up the rough stone stairs, she became aware that Niccolo's attention was solely focused upon herself. He had been a charming and courteous companion all the afternoon without attempting any familiarity other than the necessary use of her first name, but his eyes always seemed to be upon her and whenever she turned her head she met his magnetic gaze. He was studying her now with an intensity which made her feel shy, so that to break the tension which seemed to be building up between them, she forced a laugh and said provocatively:

'Is there something wrong with me?'

'Wrong? How so?'

'You always seem to be staring at me.'

'Don't you like to be admired?'

'Oh, it's admiration, is it? I thought I must have put my make-up on badly.' She moved restlessly; there was more than admiration in his dark eyes. 'I'm not unique, you must have met many pretty blonde girls in your time.'

'But none so fair as you are, *mia bianca rosa*,' he said ardently. 'Your hair, your skin, they play havoc with the senses of the dark men of the south.' He lightly touched her cheek with his finger tip. 'Your flesh is as soft as the petals of a white rose, to which I likened you. But you are so cool, so calm. Are the women of your country made of ice?'

This flowery description embarrassed her, and she moved away from him, saying over her shoulder:

'Are the men of Sicily all poets?'

She had had to deal with amorous males before, but he was in an unusual position, a connection of her employer's and at that moment posing as her husband. She dared not snub him too sharply—besides, she did not think he meant to be impertinent.

'No more than others, but lovely women have always inspired poetry,' he said gallantly. 'Your hair is like spun gold with silver light upon it. Won't you let it loose as so many girls do, to delight my eyes?'

'Sorry to disoblige you, but it's too long,' she returned. 'I'd look like a hippy.'

'A what?' The term was unfamiliar to him.

'Forget it, but please remember I'm Carlotta's nannie.'

He made an impatient gesture with one slim brown hand. 'We left her behind at the villa. Here I am speaking to my wife.'

'You know that pretence is only a security measure.'

'How prosaic you are! In this fantastic place make-believe could seem real.'

'Nannies can't afford to play such games,' she said coldly.

He gave her a languishing look. 'Don't they ever fall in love?'

'Only with their own kind.'

'How convenient, and what a fallacy.' His tone was gently mocking. 'I do not think you know anything about love. It does not confine itself to its own kind. It comes suddenly and unexpectedly to the most unlikely couples. I would like to teach you ... about love ... *mia bianca rosa*.'

His expression was beguiling, his black eyes soft as velvet. It was not fair that a man should have such beautiful eyes, she thought wildly; they could express unutterable things, which he did not mean in the least. With an effort she threw off the spell of them and retorted coldly:

'That would never do, and aren't your affections engaged elsewhere?'

His face became blank and his eyes hardened to jet.

'You must not judge by appearances,' he told her.

'I don't, but though I may be pretending to be your wife, I'd sooner you kept your distance, *signore*,' she rebuked him. 'We are here solely on Carlotta's account, and I think we should go to her.'

She moved quickly away to the steps which the child had ascended, and began to climb upwards nimbly over the stones, but she was overwhelmingly conscious of Niccolo's presence behind her. The going was rough and steep, and her concentration disturbed. The sun beat down upon her bared head, for she wore no hat and had mislaid her sunglasses. Coming to a place where the stone was broken away, she turned giddy, stumbled and swayed. She would have fallen backwards if Niccolo had not caught her with a swift agile swoop. He turned her in his arms and held her against his chest. Both were wearing the thinnest of shirts, and she could feel his warm, hard flesh against her breasts. Excitement stirred in her blood, and when he bent his head and kissed her lips, she made no resistance. The touch of his mouth was gentle and exploratory, but it awoke desire in both of them. His arms tightened, and she could feel the rapid beat of his heart above her own; almost without volition, her own arms crept about his neck, and her body seemed to melt into his. He kissed her again, and now his mouth was hot and demanding, and the buckle of the belt he wore pressed painfully into her midriff.

Something like horror overwhelmed Lucy as she suddenly realised what she was doing. She was being quite crazy to surrender to this foreign philanderer, whose motives were questionable, and in a public place too. She was behaving like some cheap little floozie he no doubt believed her to be. She wrenched herself out of his arms so violently that she nearly fell headlong down the steps, and would have done so, but for his staying hand.

'You had better take my arm,' he suggested, 'it is a rough climb and you seem none too steady on your feet.'

'I can manage,' she said breathlessly, and pulling herself free scrambled desperately up the next few steps, then, as they gained the broad aisle that swept horizontally across the theatre between the two tiers of seats, she spun round to face him, her hand to her desecrated lips.

'How dare you behave so abominably, *signore!*'

His black eyes were dancing with merriment.

'Why so outraged? Have you never been kissed before? You liked it.'

Her eyes wavered before his, and her colour rose, for she knew she had been acquiescent, if not responsive.

'That's neither here nor there,' she said disdainfully. 'You forget our respective positions.'

'I remembered only that I am a man and you are a most desirable woman. The opportunity was too good to miss.'

'Of course you would take advantage of it,' she snapped angrily, and turned her attention to the next flight of steps.

He slid his hand under her elbow and when she stiffened, told her:

'Careful now, or you may give me a further opportunity to repeat the performance.'

'Oh, I'll be careful,' she flung at him. 'I can't afford not to be!'

But she had to submit to his supporting hand, for the steps were broken and slippery, but in every nerve she was aware of the clasp of his strong brown fingers and the proximity of his hard lean body.

Carlotta had outdistanced her companions, who had
given up the climb and had reached the topmost row
of the amphitheatre. She was seated regally on the stone
bench and watched their arduous approach with imp-
ish glee.

'I go more quick than you,' she said, proud of her
achievement. She squinted up at Niccolo. 'Did you kiss
Mees because she hurt herself?'

Lucy felt ashamed as she realised Carlotta had seen
Niccolo embrace her. She was thankful for the childish
interpretation she put upon his action. He, quite at his
ease, said solemnly:

'It is the best way to heal a hurt.'

Or inflict one, Lucy thought. She was sophisticated
enough to recognise that there was a strong chemical
attraction between herself and Niccolo Martelli, and
that she would have to be on her guard if she did not
want to make a complete fool of herself. She had been
crazy to agree to this masquerade which placed her in
such a defenceless position. She vowed to herself that
this was the first and last time she would go out with
him, though how she was going to explain her reluctance to the Conte was a problem for which she must
think up some solution.

Carlotta claimed all Niccolo's attention going down,
for she was tired with her exertions, and he ended by
carrying her. Lucy followed them as best she could.
Deciding they had had enough for one day, they returned to the villa, Lucy sitting in the rear seat of the
car, with a drowsy child across her knees.

Niccolo insisted upon accompanying them up to
the nursery, saying he was staying for dinner downstairs, and wanted to see his 'family' safely bestowed

before he changed. He had a room in the house where he kept some of his clothes. This reminder of his intimate position there, and particularly with his hostess, had a salutary effect upon Lucy, effectively nipping in the bud any romantic leanings she had towards him. Physically they might be drawn to each other, but he only regarded her as a diversion when the real object of his desires was not present.

Arriving in her sitting room, they found Giulia waiting for them, and Lucy decided Carlotta had better go straight to bed and have her supper brought to her there, as she was quite exhausted by her new experiences. Her manner was frigid, for she did not want Niccolo to be encouraged to stay.

'Poor mite, she is tired,' he agreed, as Giulia took the child into the bathroom. 'But children are resilient. We will give her a day to rest and then we will go somewhere else.'

Lucy braced herself for battle. 'I think not,' she said. 'These excursions are too exhausting for so young a child. They had better be few and far between.'

'Oh, indeed?' Niccolo looked surprised. 'I thought we all enjoyed ourselves—and was not the idea yours in the first place?' He came up to her and taking her by the chin, forced her to meet his eyes. 'Aren't you being selfish and a bit of a coward, Mees Loring? Because I kissed you ...'

'Hush!' she glanced uneasily at the bathroom door.

He ignored her caution.

'Would you deprive us all of a great deal of pleasure because you chanced to fall up some steps and I forgot myself? Unless you make a habit of falling over masonry, it is not likely to occur again.'

'Thank you for that assurance,' she said sarcastically, 'but I really can't see how you can find any amusement in trailing around with a young child and her nannie.'

'Can you not?' His eyes glinted, and Lucy decided that his denial of a repetition was worthless. 'I have a great affection for the child,' he went on, 'and I can bear with the nannie for her sake.' A remark that was so unexpected that Lucy gasped. He dropped her chin and thrust his hand into his trouser pocket, his face expressionless as he proceeded to study the ceiling with a detached air. Lucy rubbed her chin where he had held it and eyed him reflectively. He seemed to have withdrawn completely and did make her opposition sound a little absurd. With his gaze still on the ceiling, he continued;

'I thought we would go next to Agrigento, the temples there are worth seeing. It is a long way, so we would have to make an early start while it is cool, and Carlotta can have a sleep in the car at midday. But if you think it would be too much for her, we will say no more about it.'

He removed his regard from the ceiling and shot her a sly glance. Lucy had been unable to restrain an eager movement. Agrigento was a place she very much wanted to see, but it was about a hundred and fifty kilometres to the west, and she had been unable to discover a bus that went there on her day off.

'The Valle dei Templi,' she murmured involuntarily.

'Exactly. Most educational.'

She shook her head. 'Don't tempt me.'

'I have every intention of trying to do so.'

Carlotta burst out of the bathroom, a curly-headed

cherub in a white nightgown, rosy and smelling of scented soap. She hurled herself at Niccolo.

'Thank you, thank you, Zio Nicco for a lovely day. You take me another time, *si*?'

'*Si, si*,' Niccolo promised, laughing, 'if your nannie agrees.'

'But Papa said ...'

'Ah, yes, Papa is on our side.' Niccolo gave Lucy a challenging look. 'Nannie must do what he tells her.'

Lucy knew she would be beaten if she appealed to the Conte. He would be scornful of any suggestion that his daughter lacked stamina, and she could not tell him her real reason for crying off. In fact she had a nasty suspicion that Niccolo's conduct was what he had anticipated. Suddenly she felt very much alone and vulnerable, caught up in a web of intrigue in which no one showed any consideration for her feelings. The Contessa resented her, the Conte was using her for his own ends, Niccolo regarded her as a diversion, and even Carlotta only tolerated her when she could get her own way. She turned away, her head drooping, swept by a wave of despondency, then pulling herself together she turned back to say to the child:

'Say goodnight to Signor Martelli and get into bed. We're going to Agrigento, but only if you're a good girl.'

She did not look at Niccolo as she made this concession, but she heard him chuckle and he said under his breath:

'And I am a good boy.'

Carlotta heard. 'You are never bad, Zio Nicco?'

'Not when I am with you, then I am at my best,' he assured her. 'Goodnight, infant.'

Gíulia, who had been cleaning up the bathroom, now appeared and smiled at Niccolo, whom she evidently admired. Carlotta gave him a wet kiss and he pushed her towards the maid with a slight grimace.

'Goodnight, Signor Martelli,' Lucy said pointedly, and moved to follow them into Carlotta's bedroom. Niccolo touched her arm to stay her.

'You have nothing to fear from me,' he told her earnestly. 'And in this house you need a friend. You can trust me.'

With a sensitivity she would not have expected in him, he had noticed her moment of despair. She gave him a grateful look and held out her hand impulsively.

'Thank you,' she said simply.

He took it and brushed her finger tips with his mouth.

'Goodnight, *bianca rosa*, sleep well.'

But after he had gone, her doubts returned. Could she trust him? Wasn't his assurance merely an attempt to lull her into a sense of false security? He was far too experienced a philanderer to scare the game in the initial stages. He persisted in calling her *bianca rosa*, which was not a correct appelation for a governess, and a little too intimate for a friend. She was confident that she could handle him in spite of her equivocal position, and after all Carlotta would be with them, but only as long as she was indifferent. The danger was her susceptibility. Exposed continuously to the seduction of those melting black eyes, that soft caressing voice, how long could her senses withstand him? However strongly reason and prudence urged her to resist? The foolish moth attracted by the flame brings about its own destruction, though if it were wise it would avoid it, but unfortunately she could not avoid Niccolo. Their encounter in the amphitheatre had shown her how vulnerable she was, and he knew it. Of his kiss he had said, 'You like it.' A statement, not a question. It was not in her nature to want to play with fire, though she knew many girls would welcome a new sensation, and to fall in love with Niccolo would be a disaster, for she could never be more to him than a plaything.

Her only hope was that he would tire of pursuing her before she capitulated, or found some other distraction. But hadn't he one already? No two women could present a greater contrast than herself and Caterina di Santa Croce. She smiled, wryly; he must like variety. But Caterina could be as vengeful as her husband, and would feel humiliated to be in competition with her own employee. Lucy gave a long sigh. Whatever happened it seemed likely her sojourn at the Villa would be brief, so she might as well make the most of it and enjoy the trip to Agrigento.

Someone has written; 'If you want to see Greece go to Sicily.' and it was at Agrigento and Selenute further west that Greek culture had left its indelible mark. There are actually two Agrigentos, the modern city on two hills and the Valle dei Templi, lapped by the sea, though the expansion of the town is reaching towards the ancient monuments.

About 500 B.C. Akragas, as it was called then, was a large, wealthy and densely populated city, but during the anti-Greek expedition of 406 B.C. the Carthaginians completely crushed it, though they left some of the temples undamaged. It revived in later times until the Arabs moved the population to its present location.

The remaining monuments were left isolated, damaged by earthquakes and plunderings, though they were not demolished to make new buildings as occurred elsewhere. Of the large Temple of Juno Lacinia, twenty-five columns survive and it stands on an eminence in solitary grandeur framed by almond trees. The Concordia Temple is almost contemporary and slightly bigger, and is practically intact. Cars were allowed within the enclosing walls, so that Carlotta's short legs were not overtaxed, as they went from ruin to ruin.

Lucy tried to envisage what they had looked like in their heyday, for what remained was only the stark skeletons, stripped of the coloured stucco decorations, chiefly in red and orange, which Niccolo told her had once embellished them, and the sculptured figures that had once adorned them. They must have been a magnificent sight.

'*Sic transit gloria mundi*,' Niccolo observed solemnly. 'The fate of all great civilisations.'

'Well, at least we're alive and able to admire them,' Lucy said cheerfully.

He looked at her significantly. 'They are a reminder to make the most of our short span until we too are with yesterday's ten thousand years.'

'By doing good deeds?' Lucy suggested.

'By snatching what joys the gods grant us.'

'You're a hedonist,' she accused him.

'There is nothing wrong with that. You take life too seriously, my little Puritan. Live, laugh and love, that is my motto.'

Lucy sighed; she had been brought up conventionally in a city suburb by conscientious parents and had

trained for a secure profession. Not much love and
laughter had come her way. She wondered if Niccolo
'loved' the Contessa. Rather like embracing a volcano,
she thought wryly, recalling her employer's sultry
brooding personality. Niccolo too suggested hidden
fires and he had complained that she herself was made
of ice. Perhaps she was, compared with these passionate
Sicilians, and she was determined she would not allow
him to melt her . . . if she could. Recalling her sensa-
tions when he had kissed her, she felt a retrospective
thrill. That might be termed living and loving, but
there would be a heavy price to pay for such indul-
gence. With uncanny perception he seemed to divine
her thoughts.

'I could teach you so much, *mia bianca rosa*,' he murmured softly, 'if only you would let me pass the barriers you persist in erecting.'

At this point Carlotta, who was becoming bored
with temples and their incomprehensible conversation,
demanded a drink. Lucy was not sorry for the interruption. Niccolo's eloquent glances were stirring
strange feelings within her which she did not want to
analyse.

They ate a picnic lunch which they had brought with
them, and then Lucy tried to persuade the child to
take a nap, but the little girl was too stimulated to
sleep. So they went up into the town, for Niccolo said
they must see the famous Phaedra's Sarcophagus in the
Diocesan Museum before they left. It was a master-
piece of Roman art, depicting the myth of Hippolytus
and the Cretan princess in high relief.

'You know the story?' Niccolo asked, as they gazed
at it.

'Vaguely. She fell in love with her stepson, didn't she?'

'Hippolytus was the son of Hippolyta the Amazon and Theseus King of Greece. She died, and Theseus married Phaedra of Crete. Hippolytus grew into a beautiful young man and Phaedra conceived a violent passion for him. He rejected her advances and in revenge she told Theseus he had raped her. Theseus cursed his son, who thereupon met a violent death. Phaedra wrote a letter exonerating him and hanged herself.' He looked away from her into the recesses of the museum. 'It is said Hippolytus made no attempt to defend himself to his father, and it is an impossible position for a man, because the husband invariably believes the wife, as in the case of Potiphar and Moses, and no man likes to betray a woman who loves him.'

Lucy wondered if he were trying to explain to her his position with regard to the Contessa, but surely he had a simple remedy. He had only to keep away from the Villa di Santa Croce. He caught her speculative glance and as if he feared he had said too much, he observed flippantly:

'These old legends have no modern counterpart, love and honour are no longer matters of life and death.'

Lucy had been long enough in the country to know that was untrue concerning honour. The Sicilian prized his very highly, and woe betide anyone who offended it. Regarding love, she was not qualified to judge, except that many people seemed to take it very lightly. She said so.

He met her eyes with a glint in his. 'Maybe, but never underrate its strength, my sleeping beauty.'

He picked up Carlotta, who was whimpering with

tiredness and wanting to go home, and said significantly over her dark head:

'You are not yet aware of your own potential, Lucy,
but sooner or later some man will wake you to it.'

But not you, she vowed silently; that would be far
too dangerous.

When they returned, the Conte was pacing the
grounds and came to meet them as they entered through
the garden door. A faint distaste wrinkled his heavy
brow as he noticed his daughter's costume, but he made
no comment, regarding it as a necessary evil. He gave
Lucy a penetrating stare and to her annoyance, she
blushed. His gaze travelled to Niccolo with a question
in it, and the younger man gave him a bland smile.

'You have been to Agrigento?' he asked. 'My wife
would like you to dine with us again, Nicco. She is
most interested to learn how ... Carlotta reacted to
the wonders of the past.'

Lucy knew very well the Contessa could not care
less; she was not concerned with her child, what she
wanted to probe was Niccolo's reaction to the nurse-
cum-governess. She could well imagine how furiously
she resented the charade she was being forced to play
with him. Surely after what he had implied at Agrigento, he would refuse the invitation? But he seemed
quite unperturbed as he accepted it graciously.

'I am always pleased to oblige the Contessa,' he said
politely.

Lucy took her charge indoors, deciding that Niccolo was a hypocrite. The Santa Croce household provided him with a convenient pied-à-terre in Syracuse
when he was in the vicinity. And had not Alfonso said
he might make him his heir? He had no intention of

avoiding either of his benefactors, and would continue to pay Caterina lip-service, if nothing else. She was inclined to think that their association went much further than that, and what was more, the Conte knew it. But curses and suicide had no part in his plans, he was much more subtle than that.

CHAPTER FOUR

NICCOLO did not suggest another expedition after Agrigento. He explained that he had to visit his vineyards at Valpena, whereupon Carlotta instantly clamoured to be taken to see them, but he said the time was not convenient; later on, perhaps.

Lucy missed his visits to the nursery; he seemed to bring sunshine with him and the days were very dull without his bright presence, though she assured herself it was better so; she was becoming far too attracted to Niccolo. Upon reflection, she decided she had read too much significance into his advances, and had made herself out to be of greater importance to him than she was. Niccolo was a flirtatious young man who had been momentarily attracted by her novelty. Sicilian unmarried girls had not yet been fully liberated and an unchaperoned, independent young woman intrigued him. But it was only a passing fancy and when he returned from Valpena he would have forgotten it, though she hoped for Carlotta's sake he would not desert them entirely. As for his affair with the Contessa, though she might deplore it; it was after all none of her business.

But the Conte seemed to be perplexed by his absence, and after several veiled hints to which she did not rise, he asked her outright if they had had a disagreement.

'No, why should we?' she replied. 'He has been a

most obliging escort, but we can't expect him to give up a lot of time to us.'

She was aware that she had coloured a little, and Alfonso gave her one of his penetrating looks.

'You expect him to return?'

'I've no right to expect anything from Signor Martelli,' she returned. 'And I don't, but Carlotta will be glad to see him again.'

'Ah, Carlotta,' the Conte exclaimed thoughtfully. 'She is an impediment, *si?*'

'I don't know what on earth you mean, *signore*,' Lucy declared, feeling uncomfortable. 'Naturally these excursions are planned for her benefit.'

'Naturally,' the Conte agreed drily.

Next day he left for Palermo on business for an indefinite period.

Though Lucy was relieved by the removal of his somewhat oppressive presence, she missed his visits, which had been a break in the monotony of their daily routine. Also in some obscure way she felt he was a protection, though she could not say against what. The weather became very warm with hot dry winds parching the country from Africa. She felt languid and Carlotta was irritable and crotchety, often demanding when Zio Nicco was coming back. That Lucy could not tell her, and it occurred to her that it was strange he continued to absent himself while Caterina was alone, then she blamed herself for her uncharitable thought.

She went out on Sunday as usual, going to Ortigia, where the Fountain of Arethusa was one of her favourite haunts. Divided from the sea by a concrete barrier, this pool of fresh water with its growth of papyrus reeds was a pleasant spot. It commemorated another

classical legend, that of the nymph Arethusa pursued
by Zeus. The obliging gods had turned her into a
fountain, and her aggressor into the river which fed it
so that their waters mingled together throughout eter-
nity ... a pretty fantasy.

From thence she ascended the steep narrow road
to the Duomo, and slipped inside to get out of the
sun. A service was going on in one of the chapels and
the drone of plainsong mingled with the scent of in-
cense. The Cathedral was remarkable because it stood
upon the site of an ancient temple dedicated to
Athene, and the original Doric columns had been in-
corporated into its outer walls. This combination of
Christian and pagan was typical of the island.

She returned home in the early evening, tired and
hot, longing for a bath and a cool drink. Entering
through the side door, to which she had a key, she ran
up the back stairs to her domain. Here to her astonishment she found the Contessa. The contents of the
nurseries had been ransacked and through her open
bedroom door she could see Giulia was packing her
cases. The writing case in which she kept her private
papers was open in front of the Contessa, the lock having been forced, and she was feverishly leafing through
the letters and documents it contained.

'*Signora!*' Lucy exclaimed, outraged by this invasion
of her privacy.

The Contessa turned a furious face towards her.

'So you have come back! I wonder at your effrontery.
Do you think I am blind to your goings on? Get out,
you viper!' She snapped the broken lock shut and rose
to her feet. 'Get out!'

Lucy glanced round. Franco was present, standing

by the window, but there was no sign of Carlotta.

'The child ...' she began.

'Ah, *mia bambina,* my little one!' The Contessa's chest heaved, but her great dark eyes were dry of tears. 'She is gone! She is taken from me!'

Lucy went cold. 'You can't mean ...?'

But she did. Carlottà had been 'snatched'.

'Oh God!' Lucy was overwhelmed. She swayed against a table, clutching it for support. 'But when and how?'

'You know that better than we do,' the Contessa said ominously. 'Stop play-acting. I always knew we should never have engaged you. Giulia has packed your things. Go before I turn you over to the police.'

'But, *signora,* I'd nothing to do with it,' Lucy cried desperately. 'I wasn't here ...'

'A blind,' Caterina declared. 'You have been with your accomplices.'

She relapsed into her own language, in which Lucy caught the words '*negligenza*' and '*tradimento*'. She glanced helplessly at Franco and saw he was looking at her accusingly. He had resented not being included in her expeditions with Niccolo, and was ready to support his mistress against her. Giulia came out of her bedroom carrying her cases, looking puzzled, but there was no sympathy in her dark eyes.

'Go!' shouted the Contessa, all the accumulated venom of the past few weeks in her face and voice. 'Never let me see you again!'

Franco came towards Lucy and rudely hustled her towards the door. The Contessa thrust her writing case at Giulia and went into Carlotta's bedroom, shutting the door, as if she could no longer bear the sight of

Lucy. Bewildered and dismayed, Lucy was conducted down the main stairway, thrust out of the front door and left standing on the doorstep with her possessions beside her. A cruising taxi spied her and drew up at the kerb.

'*Dove va, signorina?*'

At least his Italian was recognisable. Lucy thought quickly, where could she go? Foreigners in trouble appealed to their consulate, but the British one was situated in Palermo. Trains went from Syracuse to the capital and she would be able to consider her position in the sanctuary of the waiting room. She was still reeling under the awful shock of the terrible thing that had happened.

'*Mi conduca alla stazione,*' she said in her uncertain Italian. Arrived there she asked the driver to take her luggage to the *sala d'aspetto*.

A crowded railway station is not the best place for contemplation. Lucy found a seat and sat down with her possessions around her and strove to collect her bewildered thoughts. She had some money, not a great deal left out of her first month's salary, but enough to take her to Palermo. She was deeply distressed about what had happened to Carlotta, it was what her father had always feared, but she was in no way to blame. Sunday was her legitimate day off and Franco and Giulia were responsible in her absence. Not surprisingly they had been anxious to shift the blame on to her. The Contessa's accusation that she had been in league with the kidnappers was of course utterly absurd. At this point it occurred to her that there was something off-key about the proceedings. If the Contessa had really believed she was an accomplice, she would surely have turned her over to the police? There had been no evidence of the presence of the police at all. Possibly she was afraid to contact them, awaiting a demand for ransom from the kidnappers, but in that case she would have hung on to Lucy as a hostage. And her frantic search through Lucy's papers? What had she been looking for? An incriminating document or ... love-letters? Did she really imagine Niccolo would write to the nannie? She had taken advantage of her husband's absence to evict her and her methods seemed melodramatic and a little absurd, but the Contessa was a larger than life personality and jealousy was never reasonable, for Lucy could not ignore the fact that Niccolo's liking for the nursery had inflamed her.

But what had happened to Carlotta? Had her mother hidden her so that she had an excuse to get rid of Lucy? Lucy hoped so, for she could not bear to think of the child in the hands of unscrupulous rogues. She supposed that if the kidnapping was genuine and she had not been framed to suit the Contessa's devious purposes, the news would be in the papers, so she would know tomorrow. Meanwhile she must decide what she was going to do. She rose wearily to her feet, intending to discover when there was a train for Palermo.

Laden with her luggage, she came out on to the platform, to discover she had not been unremarked. A group of youths were watching her surreptitiously and saw she was alone. One of them, an impudent, swaggering fellow, came towards her and put his hand upon her larger case. She could not understand what he said, for he spoke the dialect, but there was no mistaking the expression in his eyes.

'*Mi lasci stare,*' Lucy said desperately, recalling the

words from her phrase book. '*Se ne vada.*'

But he had no intention of leaving her alone or going away. He smiled and his smile was lascivious. Lucy
looked wildly round wondering where she could get
help. There must be an official or a policeman to whom
she could appeal.

Help came—a strong muscular hand fell upon the
youth's shoulder and he was whirled to one side, her
case was snatched from his hold.

'Where are you going?' Niccolo asked.

'Oh, Nicco!' In her relief at the sight of his familiar
features Lucy addressed him informally. 'Thank God
you came!'

'He is not typical,' Niccolo told her, quick to defend
his countrymen. 'Most Sicilianos respect a lady.' He
frowned at her cases. 'Running away?'

'Well, I ...' Recollection of her predicament overwhelmed her. 'Niccolo, is it true Carlotta has been kidnapped?'

'Ssh!' he warned her, glancing at the scurrying
crowd. 'We cannot talk here.' He hefted her larger case
and reached for the smaller one. 'I have my car outside,
I can take you wherever you want to go.'

'I was intending to go to Palermo, and I can get a
train.' She did not want to be beholden to anyone connected with the di Santa Croce family, and he had
probably been told what had happened.

He shook his head. 'Not a wise choice, but come
along, we can discuss it in the car.'

He marched off with her luggage and she followed
meekly, not knowing what else to do. Why was Palermo
not a good choice? Outside was parked Niccolo's
favourite white sports car, not the more sober Fiat. He

had a triumphant air which disquieted her and his black eyes were glittering with excitement. A sudden suspicion seized her. Had he engineered Carlotta's disappearance? But what possible motive could he have in doing so?

He threw her cases in the back and indicated the passenger seat.

'Get in.'

She hesitated. 'I think ...'

'Don't think, do as you are told,' he said menacingly, and propelled her into the low seat.

He drove carefully through a maze of streets until they came to the highway to Catanza, one of the best and newest expressways in Sicily. Here he accelerated and Lucy recognised the road to the airport. Perhaps he meant to send her home by air. She said tentatively:

'Have you been deputed to deport me?'

He smiled. 'As an undesirable alien? I have no instructions to do so.' He edged carefully past a truck. 'It seems you are homeless. I am taking you to a refuge.'

'You ... you're very kind,' she told him doubtfully. 'But I don't want to impose upon you. I was going to the British Consulate at Palermo, I'm sure they'll be able to help me.'

'They are more likely to hand you over to the police for questioning.'

'Oh no! Niccolo, you aren't saying they'll think I know something about Carlotta's disappearance? I had nothing to do with it.'

'I am sure you have not, but Caterina may represent the matter in a different light. She is quite capable of telephoning them and asking them to hold you.'

'She won't know where I've gone.'

'It is the obvious place.'

'The Conte is in Palermo, you probably know where he's to be found. He will defend me.'

'Will he?'

Lucy was silent. She was by no means sure that he would. She felt trapped in a web of intrigue the object of which she could not fathom.

'But the Contessa wants me to go,' she pointed out after a pause. 'Why should she try to stop me?'

'They would probably contact her as your employer and she would not miss a chance of making trouble for you,' he told her grimly. 'That is why I said Palermo was not a wise choice. Caterina has a score to settle with you, she will not let you get away until it is settled.'

Lucy shivered. 'But you'll help me, won't you, Niccolo?' she pleaded. 'I could get a flight from Catania, if you'll lend me my fare.'

'I do not want you to leave.'

Lucy's heart gave a hard throb as she stared at his unrevealing profile. His eyes were fixed on the road ahead and a little mischievous smile curved his handsome mouth.

'Do you want to leave me?' he went on softly. 'Never see me again?'

In spite of her perturbation his words struck a responsive chord. She would hate never to see him again, but the bereft feeling his words evoked was a warning against the dangers of involvement. Much better for her peace of mind if he passed out of her life for ever.

'Whose side are you on?' she asked. 'Mine, or the Santa Croce's?'

'Neither. I play a lone hand,' he returned. 'Turning their mistakes to my advantage.'

An ambiguous statement which she did not find reassuring. It was growing dark and a fiery illumination ahead of them marked the crest of Etna, the bulk of which was obscured by the falling dusk.

'*Signore*, I'm worried about Carlotta,' she began, as her thoughts reverted to the child.

'You need not be. No Siciliano would harm a little one.'

'No? What about the Getty boy? They cut off his ear.'

'I said Sicilianos—they were Italians.'

'Aren't Sicilians Italian?'

'They are not the same, but do not trouble yourself about Carlotta, no harm will come to her.'

'You mean it's all a plot, to frame me?'

'I do not know what you mean by "frame",' he replied evasively, 'but I can tell you one thing.' His smile broadened to a grin, a flash of even white teeth in his brown face faintly lighted by the glow from the dashboard. 'Madonna la Contessa would be furious if she knew you were with me now.'

That started another train of thought.

'How did you know where to find me?' she asked.

'Giulia,' he told her. 'She saw you drive off in the taxi and guessed where you were going when she saw the direction it took.'

'I thought she was accusing me like everyone else.'

'She was puzzled, like everyone was,' he informed her. 'Except me,' he added.

'Did you have inside knowledge?' she asked scornfully.

'I'm not in Caterina's confidence, if that is what you mean, but I knew she would get rid of you on one pretext or another. You know why?'

Lucy did. 'It is all your fault,' she said severely. 'You should have kept out of the nursery.'

'Why should I be separated from Carlotta?' he asked plaintively. 'You know I am fond of her.'

'You don't seem very anxious about her.'

'I have told you there is no reason to be so.'

Lucy did not know if he really believed that or was only trying to comfort her. She leaned her head back against the headrest behind her and closed her eyes. She was very tired and she had not eaten for a long while. The afternoon by the Arethusa fountain seemed a hundred years ago. The powerful car ate up the miles of the highway and she found the motion soothing. She did not know where Niccolo was taking her, she was too weary to care greatly. There was an odd contentment in sitting beside him. Against her better judgment she felt he was a friend, her only friend in an alien, hostile land. He had told her he was and she would need him. She very definitely did.

She must have dozed, for a change in the motion of the car brought her wide awake with a jerk. They had left the highway, and the surface of this side road was not nearly so smooth. Catanza, a blaze of light in the distance, lay to one side of them while above them Etna waved a smoky plume. The road wound upwards through vineyards and groves of citrus trees, the laurel, the most common shrub in Sicily, clustered round homesteads each showing a single light. Then she knew where they were going.

'You're taking me to Valpena,' she said.

'Where else could we go?'

'I don't know.' Her eyes filled with tears. 'Carlotta so wanted to visit it.'

'So she shall . . . some day.'

'Oh, I hope so.'

'I know so.'

Lucy wished she shared his confidence. Outcast, exhausted, full of apprehension, optimism was far from her thoughts. The car turned in through a gateway, traversed a short gravelled drive and came to a halt in front of a low white house covered with bougainvillea, which gleamed crimson and purple in the car lights. Niccolo switched them off and sprang out of the car.

'Beppo! Paolina!' he called.

The house door opened and an elderly man servant hurried down the three steps which led to the front door.

'Si, signore,' he responded. 'Benvenuto, signore.'

The lighted doorway behind him framed a grey-haired woman in black peasant's garb, a shawl half over her head and draping her shoulders.

Niccolo spoke to them in Italian, then came out to help Lucy out of the car. She was so stiff she moved with difficulty and was glad of his assistance. She stood swaying in the driveway while Niccolo took out her cases which the man Beppo picked up.

'Paolina speaks some English,' Niccolo told her, taking her arm and guiding her towards the open door. 'She will show you the guest room and run you a bath. Then we will eat . . . and talk.'

Lucy went where she was led, moving like someone in a dream. The house had none of the grandeur of the

Villa di Santa Croce, but she was only vaguely aware of her surroundings. The small low-ceilinged room into which she was conducted smelt of roses and lavender. The window, to which was fixed the usual iron balcony, looked down the slope to a mass of vine-yards.

Paolina helped her off with her clothes and into the scented bath in an adjoining bathroom. The warm water revived her. Wrapped in the big fleecy towel provided for her, she re-entered the bedroom to find Paolina had unpacked her cases and laid out clean underwear and one of her white dresses. She looked longingly at the divan bed, wanting to sleep and sleep, but first she had to face Niccolo. She was suspicious of his motives in bringing her here and she prayed he was not going to be difficult, for she felt unequal to dealing with an amorous male in her weary state. While she brushed and combed her hair, the woman brought her a glass of wine on a salver. Lucy looked at it doubtfully; it would probably go to her head and she needed to keep her wits about her.

'Drink,' said Paolina. She did speak English, but with a heavy accent. 'Do you good.'

Lucy decided that she did need some stimulant to meet whatever lay ahead of her. The wine was a sweet Marsala, product of the country, and a little heavy. She put down the empty glass, feeling new life flow through her veins.

There was a tap on the door.

'*Avanti!*' Paolina called without asking for Lucy's permission.

Niccolo stood on the threshold arrayed in a white silk shirt, black trousers and, a barbaric touch, a scarlet sash about his middle. He had bathed and shaved, his thick dark hair slicked down and looked sleek and, alas, overwhelmingly attractive. Lucy felt her heart turn over at the sight of him.

She was seated in front of the looking glass on a low stool in her blue negligee with her loosened hair falling about her face and shoulders, the brush in her hand, her sleeve falling back from one slim pale arm as she held it arrested in the act of applying it to her hair. She made an alluring picture in pale blue and gold, and Niccolo's eyes glinted, his nostrils dilated slightly as he beheld her.

'*Bella*, Paolina, is she not?' There was all the pride of possession in his voice as he spoke to the woman.

Paolina's seamed face set in lines of disapproval.

'*Molta bella, signore*, but zis one *e vergine*.'

Niccolo looked startled. 'How do you know that?'

Paolina shrugged her shoulders, and taking the brush from Lucy began to brush her hair with long smooth strokes. The pale gold mass spun out in silver-gilt spray as she did so and Niccolo audibly caught his breath, but when he spoke it was formally.

'Food has been prepared for us in the *sala di pranzo*. You will come down, *si*?'

'In a minute,' Lucy told him. 'As you can see, I'm not quite dressed.' There was rebuke in her voice for his intrusion upon her toilet.

'Forgive me,' he said humbly, but there was no humility in his expression. 'I should have waited until you endorsed Paolina's permission. She sees no need for formality between us and I have her to thank for a sight of your beautiful hair unbound. Won't you leave it so while we dine?'

A coaxing note crept into his voice, but Lucy had no intention of yielding to his request. She knew that he had always been fascinated by her hair, but her position was quite equivocal enough without adding to its provocation.

'It would get into the food,' she pointed out. 'I will be with you in five minutes, *signore*.'

'It was Niccolo in the car,' he reminded her.

'Then I was not quite myself,' she retorted.

'And now you are? How unfortunate!'

'Please, *signore*,' her long grey eyes were pleading. 'I'm very tired. I can't bandy words with you tonight.'

'Who wants you to, poor little one? You will find me . . . all solicitude. *Arrivederci, bianca rosa.*'

He was gone, and Paolina tight lipped laid down the brush.

'You *il signore*'s woman?' she asked bluntly.

'No.' Lucy began to twist her hair into a tight knot at her nape. 'I'm on my way back to England, but there was a delay, and Signor Martelli offered me hospitality, until I can get a flight.'

It sounded lame, but what could she say? She should have insisted upon going to Palermo, but Niccolo's warning had frightened her. Would she really be turned over to the police? But if Carlotta was safe as he had insisted, of what could she be accused? She felt she was the victim of some sort of conspiracy, the object of which was obscure.

Paolina slipped the white dress over her shoulders, it was plain and simple, and she certainly did not look in the least like a tart. Impelled by an unworthy curiosity, she asked:

'Does Signor Martelli often bring women here?'

Paolina gave an Italian shrug. 'Wat would you? E ees young and virile. E should 'ave a wife.'

Carlotta, for whom he must wait so many years? Recollection of the child caused her lip to quiver. If only she were with her here now! She wondered if the woman knew what was supposed to have happened, but the Sicilian's small dark eyes were unrevealing. Probably not, there had not been time for the news to be publicised. But if it were all a hoax, it never would be.

'Please show me the way to the dining room,' she requested.

It was not very large, none of the rooms in the house were, its windows opened on to a paved terrace facing the same direction as her bedroom did, as she could see for the curtains were undrawn. The walls were plain colour wash in pale ochre, with several framed water colours. The furniture, sideboard, oval table and chairs were in dark wood, and the room was lighted by candles in heavy silver candlelabra, the flames of which were reflected in the polished surface of the table set with lace mats, silver and cut glass wine glasses. Beppo in an ancient black cutaway coat waited upon them. They were served lasagne followed by fish of some Mediterranean variety, cheese and fruit. The wine was Asti Spumante, and forgetting her caution, Lucy allowed her glass to be filled twice. She liked sparkling wine and Niccolo's sensuous glances excited her out of her normal prudence. While the manservant was in the room he confined himself to glances, his conversation being about the locality and its people. As he had already told her the land on the slopes of the volcano was very fertile. Prickly pear, almonds, olives, pistachios and dense orange groves flourished on the *terra forti*, where centuries-old lava had fertilised the ground. Higher up where his land was situated, grew flowers and orchards of apples, pears, cherries and vines. Higher still were forests. Etna covered a vast area, nearly two thousand square kilometres. The snow lingered on it for six months of the year, and the ascent to the craters was quite a feat, the quickest way being from Catania to Nicolosi, a tourist resort nearby from which a cable car went up to the main crater, but it was essential to have a guide over the treacherous lava and minor craters.

Lucy listened enthralled as he went on to describe the summit, the fine view from it, and the lunar scenery. The 1971 eruption had destroyed an observatory and the upper stretch of the cableway, but that had been a comparatively minor one. It would probably do the same again ere long.

'Is Catania in any danger?' she asked.

He smiled. 'Volcanoes are unpredictable. In 1669 Etna did damage it, but earthquakes are a greater hazard. The one in 1639 practically destroyed the city.'

'I'm glad I live in a temperate climate,' Lucy said with a shiver.

'You are not in a temperate climate now.' Niccolo's smile was significant. 'There are other subterranean fires besides volcanic ones in this country.'

His eyes smouldered, and Lucy thought, 'Oh, lord, now it's coming!' But Beppo came in to tell them coffee was served in the *salotto*.

'Might I be excused?' Lucy asked. 'I ... I'm awfully tired, and I don't want any coffee.'

'You may not,' Niccolo told her with a sudden tightening of his jaw muscles. 'Do not pretend your dinner has not revived you. You will hurt Beppo's feelings if you do not sample his coffee.' He ushered her to the door. 'The *salotto* is in here.' He indicated the next room. 'Afterwards, *amore mia*, you shall sleep, in my arms the whole night through.'

CHAPTER FIVE

LUCY managed to precede Niccolo into the adjoining room with an appearance of calm, disguising the mingling of panic and excitement his devastating remark had caused her.

The *salotto* was also candlelit, and with the long silk curtains drawn over the window, its luxurious settee and arm chairs, and vases of roses the scent of which perfumed the air, it looked like a stage set for a seduction scene. The coffee pot was placed on a low table in front of the settee.

She supposed the present situation was inevitable, everything Niccolo had done and said since meeting her on the station platform had been leading up to it, perhaps even long before, from the moment she had met his dark eyes over the Contessa's sofa. He was confident of her surrender and had some cause to be, since there was that between them which would not make resistance easy, but resist him she was determined to do. Her pride revolted from being used as an assuagement of his frustration over Caterina. She did not believe he would try to force her, but he would do his utmost to persuade her, and with all his physical advantages, he could be very persuasive indeed.

She walked without faltering to the chesterfield and sat down upon it behind the coffee set, while Niccolo shut the door firmly and locked it. The click of the turning key was an ominous sound, and Lucy felt a little sick in the pit of her stomach caused by her deep despondency. He had seemed to be a possible friend in a world that had turned suddenly hostile, and now he had ranged himself with her enemies.

'White or black?' she asked composedly, preparing to pour out the coffee; it would give her something to do while she summoned her resources to face the ordeal to come.

Niccolo seemed disconcerted by her self-possession, as if he had expected his remark to have thrown her into a welter of quivering anticipation. He glanced at her obliquely, wondering if she had heard him or had misunderstood his intention.

'Black,' he told her, 'with plenty of sugar.'

She managed the operation without a tremor and handed him his cup with a steady hand, only her pallor betraying her inner turmoil. She dared not look at him, though her every nerve was aware of him and his olive face and graceful figure so well displayed by his slightly theatrical attire was imprinted upon her inner vision. She busied herself with her own drink, though when she took a sip of it she tasted nothing. To her relief Niccolo had not sat down beside her but perched himself on the arm of the chair opposite to her.

Niccolo swallowed his coffee, and then set his cup down upon the table with a violence that caused it to rattle.

'*Dio mio*, this is absurd! You sit there so prim and proper as if I was an infant in your nursery and you were about to tell me not to gulp my drink. Little gentlemen should take it slowly and make polite conversation between sips.' He spoke with savage mockery.

'Are you flesh and blood, you little icicle? Here we
are alone together at last and you try to freeze me.
Madonna mia, I will make you burn for me!'

He sprang to his feet but he did not touch her. He
stood flexing his fingers, while his narrowed eyes glit-
tered between his half closed lids. Lucy said bitingly:

'I should have known there would be a price to pay
for your hospitality.' Her lip quivered and tears started
to her eyes. 'Oh, Nico, I thought better of you. You
told me I could trust you.'

His eyes widened in astonishment.

'But, *amore mia*, do you not want to sleep with me?'
I have seen the desire in your eyes in response to mine.
Do not pretend to be shy—I know better than that.'

He dropped into the seat beside her on the chesterfield. His hands went to her head to release her hair
and it fell around her like a cloak. He ran his fingers
through its meshes with sensuous enjoyment.

'Like silk,' he murmured. 'How I have longed to do
this—and you are so unkind to keep it knotted up.'
He gathered up a handful and drew it across his lips.
Through its strands his eyes sought hers.

'I will not hurt you, *bianca rosa*, I am a very prac-
tised lover, I will give you much pleasure.'

'You flatter yourself!' Her wide grey eyes met his
brilliant dark gaze courageously while she strove to
subdue the wild beating of her heart. 'I suppose you
think that because I'm a dependant in the Conte's
household and have been disgraced, you need not show
me respect.'

'Respect?' he smiled. 'What a cold word! You do
not need respect, you were made for love, *mia bella*,
and it is no compliment to you to hold aloof. *Dio mio*,

how I have longed to hold you in my arms and melt that little cold heart, and now I have you here in my house, with no one to come between us.'

Lucy glanced wildly round the room and her eyes lighted on the heavy brass candlesticks, set on the mantelshelf above a grate disguised by a pot plant. Whisking her hair out of his fingers, she jumped to her feet and seized one of them.

'Touch me and I'll brain you!' she threatened.

Niccolo lunged after her, laughing, and seized her wrist in a vicelike grip which caused her to drop the candlestick on the floor. The candle spluttered and died, leaving the room even dimmer than before.

'Better and better, so you would provoke me, would you, pretending to be the little wildcat? *Carissima*, it will be much pleasure to tame you.'

He sank back on to the chesterfield, pulling her down across his knees, his other arm encircled her like a coiling snake, and like a snake he tightened his hold to a painful constriction. Freeing her wrist, his hand pulled at the zip which fastened the front of her dress, exposing her chest naked but for her bra. Outrage at this violation battled with Lucy's rising excitement. She turned her head away from his seeking mouth and gasped:

'Isn't the Contessa enough for you? Let me go!'

He slackened his hold while he stared into her white face.

'I have never been her lover and never will be.'

Lucy did not believe him; what she had seen at the Villa indicated otherwise.

'The first time I saw you you were paying court to her,' she accused him, 'and you're always at the Villa.'

'Papa instructs me in his business, and the wheels run smoother if I pay Caterina the little attentions. But Alfonso di Santa Croce is my benefactor and his honour is safe in my keeping.'

'Is it indeed?' she said scornfully. 'And my honour is of no account?'

'But you are *Inglesa*, *permessa*, why should I consider it?'

He dropped his head and began to kiss her neck and breasts, but his contemptuous words had frozen her into a cold fury. She became rigid in his arms and when he sought her lips she closed them firmly. Niccolo lifted his head with a puzzled frown.

'I do not please you?'

'Not when you treat me like a tart! I'm a good girl, Nicco.'

'You mean Paolina was right when she said you are *una vergine*?'

'But of course I am.'

'It is not possible.'

His arms went slack and she slid off his knees, hastily pulling up her zip.

'It's perfectly possible. Because I work for my living it doesn't mean I'm available for all and sundry.'

She stood before him, her arms crossed over her bosom and there was that in her eyes which convinced him. It explained the lack of response which he had expected. He got up and faced her frowning perplexedly.

'But your parents? You have parents, *si*?'

'Yes, I've got parents, very respectable ones,' she told him drily. If they could see her now they would believe she was completely abandoned; they had not approved of her decision to take a situation abroad and they would feel that all their objections were proved justified. But she had never contemplated encountering anyone like Niccolo.

'Then how come they permit?' he asked.

'I'm of age, I don't have to ask their permission as to what I do.'

'But a beautiful girl like you should be guarded.'

'Oh, rubbish, you seem to be still in the Dark Ages out here. Don't you know modern girls go out to work without supervision? I'm a trained children's nurse and I fancied a job abroad, but I wish I hadn't chosen Sicily.'

Her voice quivered on the last sentence and she drooped like a bruised lily as the realisation of her precarious position struck her with added force. The child in her charge was alleged to have been kidnapped, herself evicted and abducted by this amorous Sicilian whom she had hoped would befriend her and was now proving the greatest danger of all.

'That was your fate,' Niccolo told her. Arab influence still lingered in the country, and he, like many others, firmly believed in destiny. 'You chose Sicily and so you come to me. Our meeting was preordained.'

'By the agency that found me the job?' she asked sarcastically.

'All that is over,' he declared dramatically. 'Henceforward I will provide for you, you will never need to work again.'

'But I like my work,' she protested, 'and I won't be a kept woman, Nicco.'

'You will be my *amore*,' he said earnestly. 'I know that the modern freedom *signorinas* all have boy-

friends, as you call them. That you have not had one
is my good luck.' His face broke into a slow triumphant
smile. 'So I will be the first,' he said with satisfaction,
'and who knows, perhaps the last. Forgive me that I
was rough, *cara*, I did not understand, but now I will
be gentle. You are ripe for love and I will teach you
how it must be, controlling my ardour until you are
ready to meet it.'

Lucy wet her lips nervously with her tongue. Niccolo's voice was soft and soothing, and stretching out
a hand, he drew her gently down beside him on the
couch. His experienced hands moved lightly over her
body, stroking, caressing, touching the erotic spots.
Her blood took fire under this treatment and a slow
dark tide of passion began to submerge her. Her resistance changed to submission, and her arms went involuntarily round his neck. She was no longer capable
of coherent thought, all she knew was that she wanted
Niccolo in every fibre of her being. Slowly he enclosed
her in his arms, and by delicious degrees increased
their pressure until she was crushed against his chest
Only then did he seek her lips, and they were parted
and eager to receive his kiss.

Someone knocked loudly on the door, and rattled the
handle.

Niccolo swore. 'Go away!' he shouted.

The knocking continued.

'*Signore*,' Beppo's old man's voice made shrill by
consternation reached them through the panels, and
he shook the door. '*Signore, il Conte* has come!'

Niccolo thrust Lucy's quivering body away from him
and strode to the door. He unlocked it, saying, 'Keep
him out of here, Beppo.'

He was too late. Alfonso di Santa Croce was standing on the threshold, a thin smile on his lips.

'What do you want, Papa?' Niccolo demanded roughly. 'As you see I am ... occupied. I thought you were in Palermo.'

'I was, but I concluded my business earlier than expected.' He deliberately switched on the light and advanced into the room. Lucy had retreated as far as the window, and was trying to bundle up her hair. The bright light made her wince. Every detail of the room would be revealed to him, and her own dishevelment.

He fixed his eyes upon her, as he went on.

'I arrived home this evening to be met with the news that my daughter had been snatched, and you, Mees Lor-ring, dismissed on the spot for conspiring with her abductors. Needless to say I was ... surprised.'

Though his voice and his face were expressionless there was deadly menace in his hooded eyes, and Lucy turned cold. What hideous vengeance would he exact for her supposed negligence? Nevertheless, knowing herself innocent, she faced him bravely.

'*Signore*, I know nothing about it. I wasn't even there, as you must know. Sunday is my day off.'

'And thus provided yourself with an alibi. It was you who wanted to take Carlotta out, so she should be easily recognisable. Also it was your idea to use the garden door which you left unlocked when you went out on Sunday morning for your confederates to enter by. You told them how to gain access to the child's quarters up the backstairs, and when your evil plan was successful you had the effrontery to return to the villa, pretending innocence. Naturally my wife threw you out at once and your baggage with you. I was a fool to engage you and a still greater one to trust you. Now we are deprived of our child through my folly.'

Lucy was horrified as she realised the logic of the case against her. Guiltless though she was, she might be condemned by circumstances. She glanced from the Conte's set face to Niccolo and saw to her astonishment that he was laughing. and a wave of furious indignation swept through her.

'I don't see anything to laugh at,' she cried. 'Is it my predicament or Carlotta's that amuses you? I thought you were fond of the child.' She turned to the Conte. '*Signore*, none of what you said is true. I love Carlotta, I'm terribly distressed by what has happened ...' She broke off, for the Conte no longer looked accusing.

'Of course it is not true. I am merely repeating the preposterous story with which my wife presented me. She said she had not had you arrested, Mees, for fear of aggravating the kidnappers, but there were no kidnappers; she had sent Carlotta to her aunt in Taormina. I got the truth out of her in the end. She was taken unawares by my unexpected return and had not had time to suborn witnesses to corroborate her tale.'

'Oh, I'm so glad Carlotta's safe,' Lucy said fervently.

'I suspected something like this,' Niccolo informed them. 'That is why I was not upset, Lucy. Had I believed Carlotta was really kidnapped, I would have torn the place apart to find her.'

'And thereby increased her danger, you young hothead,' the Conte reprimanded him, but his eyes twinkled. 'And I must thank you for succouring Mees Lor-ring. How did you find her?'

'I thought she would make for Palermo and the British Consulate there and I picked her up at the station, but how did you discover she was here?'

'I too deduced that she would make for Palermo and when I enquired at the station, someone had recognised you and saw you leave with a lady. Of course you would bring her here.'

That recalled Lucy to her compromising situation and she blushed fierily.

'I ... I didn't know where to go,' she faltered. 'Nic ... Signor Martelli warned me that the Contessa might put the police on to me if I showed up at the consulate.' She looked at Niccolo reproachfully. 'You knew perfectly well there was no danger of that.'

'No, I did not. I did not know for certain that nothing had happened to Carlotta, though, begging your pardon, Papa, I was fairly sure it was all a plot of Caterina's to get rid of Lucy.'

'Which she has done,' the Conte remarked, and Lucy's heart sank. Innocent she might be, but she could not return to the villa. In other words, the Contessa had won.

'I'll have to go back to England,' she said despondently.

'Oh no, you will stay with me,' Niccolo declared.

Lucy forgot the presence of the Conte. 'Nicco, I can't be your mistress,' she said firmly, because that was what he meant. 'I ... I thank you, it's a sort of compliment really, but I keep telling you I'm not that sort of girl.'

'But you are human and a woman. I will protect you, look after you, give you everything you desire,' he said earnestly.

The Conte cleared his throat, and Lucy was abashed to realise he had overheard Niccolo's words. Not so his stepson. He had made what he considered was a reasonable and generous offer and saw no need to be ashamed of it.

Alfonso smiled wryly. 'You are forgetting Mees Lorring is a virtuous woman,' he remarked. 'She has just proved it. As such I respect her. You can do better than that, Nicco.'

The young man looked bewildered. 'How so, Papa?'

'I should prefer to be able to receive her in my house,' his stepfather went on blandly. 'And you will want to see Carlotta again, won't you, my dear? But she can only do so if she is ... ahem ... respectable.'

'You know very well Caterina will continue to vilify her whatever she does,' Niccolo declared.

'Not if she has the protection of your name,' the Conte said suavely, and as both Niccolo and Lucy gaped at him, his glance sharpened to steel. 'In honour bound we owe Mees some reparation. I suggest—no, I command, that you marry her.'

Lucy stared at him blankly. She had always been aware that from the moment the Conte had first set eyes upon her he had intended to use her to drive a wedge between his stepson and his wife, but that he would carry his intention to the point of ordering a marriage between them was so improbable she felt completely baffled. For he had told her himself that for lack of a son he might make Niccolo his heir, and members of the Sicilian aristocracy did not marry impecunious English nannies. Her eyes went to Niccolo and she saw he looked taken aback. He had been quite willing to pretend to be her husband, and had got a kick out of acting the part, but the reality was another matter. When circumstances played into his hands, he had been eager to make her his mistress, but obviously the thought of marriage had never crossed his mind. He was looking in perplexity at his benefactor.

'Is that really your wish, Papa?'

'You are ungallant,' came the stern reply. 'Lucia,' he used the Italian form of Lucy's first name, and that he did use it showed he was prepared to accept her, 'will not be flattered by your hesitation.'

'Ah, forgive me.' The dark eyes flashed to Lucy with an almost inimical look in their velvet depths. 'Of course I am delighted at the prospect of so fair a bride.'

But the glib words were mechanical and Lucy gained the impression that Niccolo was secretly dismayed by the Conte's decree. Though he had played along with his stepfather willingly when his object had been seduction, he shrank from the marriage tie, or so she interpreted his apparent reluctance.

It was ironic that Caterina's plotting had created a situation which she would be the first to deplore, and that was what was galling Lucy. The Conte was prepared to go to any lengths, even to admitting a little nobody into his exclusive family, to end the liaison which he suspected existed between Niccolo and his wife, and to expose Caterina to the pangs of jealousy and despair which this marriage would cause her. A true Sicilian vengeance, but he might be too optimistic. If the couple really were lovers there was no reason why a marriage to Lucy should be a barrier, any more than the Contessa's own marriage appeared to be. The Conte probably thought that a young and pretty bride would detach Niccolo from his former inamorata, but Lucy was not so sure. She might even be used as a cover for their intrigue if the Conte's suspicions were lulled, and she could not lend herself to such a humiliating position.

The Conte was not at all put out by Niccolo's lack of enthusiasm, it was probably what he expected, but Lucy found it painful. It would seem to indicate he had no real love for her.

'You have wine here?' the Conte enquired, looking about him. 'Let us drink to celebrate your betrothal, my dear boy.'

The look the two men exchanged was like crossed swords. Then Niccolo laughed mirthlessly.

'Since you have anticipated my wooing, I can only concur,' he said lightly. He went to a cupboard in the wall and produced a bottle and glasses. He poured the red wine into them and handed one to Lucy. It was, she noticed, the colour of blood. Heart's blood—Niccolo's? Caterina's? Or hers? She put it down on the table.

'I haven't given my consent,' she said stonily. 'I can't marry Niccolo.'

The Conte stared at her in astonishment, his eyes for once fully revealed.

'Why ever not?'

'It's ... it's obvious we're unsuited,' she returned, 'and ... and he doesn't love me.' She glanced at Niccolo hopefully, but his face was unresponsive. The Conte laughed and snapped his fingers.

'Bah, what bagatelle is this? I find you both here behind a locked door and you complain that he does not love you!' He stared pointedly at Lucy's loosened hair which was falling about her shoulders. 'Do you not understand, Lucia?—we are offering you wealth, position and in time, a title.'

Niccolo uttered an exclamation, and Lucy knew he was being bribed by the sure promise of what had previously been only a supposition.

She shook her head. 'Such things don't appeal to me, and they can't compensate for ... for happiness.'

Niccolo cried arrogantly, 'Of course I would make you happy.'

Had they been alone she would have told him frankly that she could not be happy if she had to share him with another woman, a woman moreover who hated her, and would miss no opportunity to denigrate her. Only his assurance that his heart was wholly hers would satisfy her, and then she would have to be convinced that he meant what he said. At that moment she felt sure he had only accepted her out of necessity. She looked at him sorrowfully. 'I don't want to marry you as a ... an expediency.'

The Conte intervened. 'Then you do realise your awkward position, Lucia? Have you fully considered the alternative? I will not permit you to stay here, I have a moral obligation towards you, but you will return to England disgraced. Oh, the kidnapping charge is absurd, of course, but my wife will consider it is her duty to inform the agency who recommended you that you are unreliable. You neglected your duties to run after men, in fact she may consider your parents should be told of your behaviour. You may find it difficult to deny that you used my daughter as a pretext for going out with my stepson.' Lucy stared at him blankly, and he smiled thinly. 'In fact, I had to send Carlotta away to be out of reach of your pernicious influence and I found you here, blatantly trying to seduce my heir.'

Lucy wilted under the stony gaze of those basilisk

eyes. The Conte would be merciless to anyone who thwarted him and the story he threatened to circulate about her would be difficult to refute. Her conventional parents would be horrified and she could not entirely deny it, for she had been discovered in Niccolo's house and if the Conte had not interrupted them, she would be by now on her way to his bed.

She covered her face with her hands as a little despairing cry broke from her.

'Oh, *signore*, you're cruel!'

'Only to my enemies, and I would be your friend,' he told her implacably. 'If you will do as I wish.'

She had almost forgotten Niccolo during this exchange, and now he came to her and put a protective arm across her shoulders.

'That will do, Papa,' he said to the older man. 'I would not have my little bride bullied into matrimony. Little one,' his tone was lightly caressing, 'you see there are worse fates than having to accept me for your husband. After all, we got along very well together when it was makebelieve, will the reality be so hard to bear?' He ran his fingers through her hair which had defied her hasty efforts to confine it. 'You were on the point of yielding to me, but would not your prim little soul rejoice if the surrender is made legitimate?'

His voice became half mocking, and lifting her head Lucy looked searchingly into his eyes. They were opaque and unrevealing and his mouth curled sardonically. He knew they were both in a trap. If he offended the Conte he would lose his hoped-for inheritance and she, if she remained obdurate, her good name, which the poet said was poverty indeed. She gave a long sigh.

'You'll be kind to me, Nicco?'

'That will be easy *bianca rosa*.'

'I take it,' the Conte's voice was sarcastic, 'this touching scene indicates that you are both prepared to obey me. So I will drink the delayed toast. Felicitations.'

He drained his glass.

Niccolo put hers into Lucy's hand and raised his own.

'To your good health and happiness, *carissima*, and please to drink to mine.'

Carissima—love words tripped so glibly off his tongue His stepfather had made it worth his while to marry her and that he found her desirable was an added bonus, but it was a long way from love. Lucy's eyes were fathomless grey pools as she drank the wine regarding him steadily over the rim of her glass. She did not really know him at all, only his glamorous outer shell. She did not speak, and he enquired reproachfully:

'Don't you wish me to be happy?'

'I'm sure you'll find happiness in obeying your stepfather's wishes,' she told him ambiguously.

'It is late,' the Conte reminded them. 'I presume you can find me a bed for the night, Nicco? Lucia, you had better retire. There are a few matters I wish to discuss with my stepson before I sleep.'

'Yes, I'm very tired,' Lucy said plaintively. All the passion Niccolo had aroused in her had drained away, leaving her exhausted. 'Goodnight *signori*.'

She inclined her head towards the Conte and went towards the door. Niccolo hurried after her to open it for her, and as she passed him, asked:

'As your *fidanzato* don't I rate a goodnight kiss?'

'I believe respectable Italian girls don't kiss their

fiancés until after they're married,' she returned.

'But you are English ...'

The Conte cut in. 'She is quite right, Nicco, you must restrain yourself from now on until after the marriage.'

Niccolo threw her a comical look of mock despair. 'So near and yet so far,' he complained. '*Buona notta, amore mia*, dream of me.'

'Goodnight again.' Lucy went swiftly through the door and made her way upstairs. The Conte was running no risk of Niccolo's ardour fading before he was safely shackled.

CHAPTER SIX

TIRED though she was, Lucy could not sleep; she was over-fatigued and over-stimulated, so that her strung nerves could not relax. Her bed was comfortable, but even the aspirin which she always carried with her had no effect. She heard the men come upstairs and pass her door. The Conte's tread was heavy, and firm, but Niccolo moved like a cat. She would not have known he was there but for the mingling of their voices.

She thought he might come to her, in spite of the Conte's veto, and half hoped, half dreaded that he would. Her resistance was at a low ebb and her body craved for him. It might be as well to let him have his way and then perhaps he would help her to escape. For she was certain he did not want to marry her, and that being so her pride revolted from being forced upon him. Though she knew she was in love with him, that was not quite the same thing as loving him. There were aspects of him which she distrusted. He was a foreigner and a Sicilian at that, brought up in a culture and tradition very different from her own. Being a level-headed young woman she knew that their union would face tremendous risks, unless there was between them a real and lasting love, and he had told her that in Sicily divorce was not recognised. He would neglect her once the first rapture was past, and even that would be spoiled by the heavy hand of the Conte. For resentment at being compelled to marry her would in-

evitably take the edge off his desire. The prospect of a
lonely life in an alien country was not at all inspiring.
No, she resolved, she could not, would not marry
Niccolo Martelli. Yet the thought of being parted from
him for ever was hard to bear. He filled her imagination and was under her skin. It would be like wrench-
ing off a limb, but it would have to be done for both
their sakes. Better a short, sharp agony than a lifetime
of regret.

What was to become of her in the immediate present,
she did not know. The Conte would not allow her to
remain at Valpena, so it would seem he intended to
take her back to Syracuse. It was part of his plan to
flaunt her under his wife's nose as Niccolo's fiancée,
and it would implement his revenge to lodge her in the
same house as the Contessa and make her participate
in the arrangements for the wedding. That seemed
only too probable, and Lucy shrank in every quivering
nerve from the prospect.

Then it occurred to her that if she wanted to escape,
she might be able to enlist Caterina as an ally. The
Contessa could give her the necessary testimonial to
enable her to obtain another job, which her husband
had threatened to withhold if she were obdurate, and
more important, could assist her to leave the country.
Though she was the last person Lucy would choose as
a conferedate it seemed she was her only hope.

Lucy smiled wryly in the darkness. The Conte was
using her to revenge himself upon his wife, for her
suspected infidelity, but she would use Caterina's
jealousy to effect her release. That Niccolo would
continue his affair with her as soon as Lucy had gone,
she feared was inevitable ... or was it? Uneasily she

recalled Niccolo's words by the Roman tomb at Agrigento. He had indicated that there was a parallel between himself and the story of Phaedra and Hippolytus, as if he wished to vindicate himself in her eyes, and by running away she would expose him to further temptation, but it might be he had been throwing dust in her eyes because he wanted to seduce her and thought she might be repelled if she believed he were Caterina's lover.

A tide of revulsion submerged her; she was sickened by these unscrupulous Sicilians and their cunning intrigues. She wanted no more to do with any of them, and she began to think of her parents and her home, which now seemed to be a haven of security. With her mind dwelling upon green fields and grey skies, she slept at last.

She was awakened before dawn by a knocking upon her door, and startled, became wide awake, for a moment at a loss as to her whereabouts. The knocking continued and her heart turned over. Niccolo? But he would not knock, he would walk straight in, for she had not locked the door, there was no key.

'Yes, what is it?' she called.

Niccolo answered it. 'Etna is putting on a little firework display and we thought you would like to see it.'

'Oh, I would!' She reached for her wrap, the same blue negligee she had worn in Syracuse. She had forgotten that the house was situated on the slopes of a volcano, the subterranean fires of which were typical of the island and its inhabitants, she thought wryly as she tied the belt of her robe. With her hair loose about her shoulders she went to open the door.

Niccolo was standing in the passage and also his

stepfather. Both men were wearing dark silk dressing
gowns and had blue chins. It was the first time she had
seen Niccolo not immaculately shaven, and that and
his rumpled hair made him seem more natural, less like
the smooth sophisticate of whom she was secretly a
little in awe.

She saw the sensual gleam in his eyes as he beheld her
deshabille, and he murmured softly:

'Ivory, gold and azure.' Then, louder for the Conte's
benefit and impersonally: 'Come out on to the balcony at the back of the house,' and led the way, careful,
she noticed, not to touch her.

The dark bulk of the mountain rose up before them
as they stepped out on to the balcony; a lurid glow
hung over its summit, illuminating what might be
clouds or smoke above it. Then from one of the craters
long fingers of fire shot up into the sky, to fall in a
rain of gold and scarlet sparks. They rose and fell
like a succession of rockets. The rim of the crater itself shone with lurid intensity. Occasionally a zig-zag
of flame ran down the side of the mountain to lose itself
in darkness.

'Is there any danger?' Lucy asked nervously, for
majestic as the spectacle was, it was full of hidden
menace.

'No, there is no lava flow, it is a jet of incandescent
lapilli erupting from an active cone,' the Conte reassured her.

Niccolo standing close beside her, slipped a protective arm around her waist. She became acutely conscious of him as his hand moved upwards over her thin
robe and closed over her breast. Her heart started the
usual antics that his touch always caused, and she drew

her breath with difficulty.

'Even if it does start erupting, we are a long way away,' he told her. 'And it might not come in this direction, but I do not think it means business tonight.'

His breath stirred her hair, and he pressed her closer to his side as, his voice sinking to a low murmur, he went on: 'There is fire in my veins too, *cara mia*, and only you can assuage it.'

After first giving it release, Lucy thought fearfully, sensing the primitive passions of the man who held her, which normally he concealed beneath a cool exterior. The same violence was hidden in his stepfather. Like the volcano it lay latent under their civilised manners, but it would erupt when love or hate provoked it.

'I don't think I would care to live with it,' she said in a stifled voice, for her own emotions were excited by his close hold, but whether she meant Etna or his temperament was not apparent, and his response to her words could answer either.

'You would come to accept it as a fact of life.'

The mountain rumbled and a molten mass shot up into the air to describe a glittering parabola through the air and a burst of flame marked where it fell.

'Only some dead trees,' the Conte said, as Lucy gave an involuntary cry.

Niccolo's arm tightened around her, as he laughed exultantly. 'Is anything more beautiful than fire?'

'Or more destructive,' Lucy whispered.

The mountain seemed to have expended its energies for that night, as no more rocket beams rose from the crater, and the dawn began to lighten the darkne behind it.

'We had better go back to bed,' the Conte decided.
He glanced sharply at their entwined figures. 'I will
escort Lucia, Nicco, it will be more seemly.'

Niccolo removed his arm with a short laugh.

'You do not trust me, Papa?'

'Can you trust yourself?' his stepfather retorted. 'The
firework display has excited you.'

He drew Lucy's arm through his, preparatory to
leading her away. It was now light enough to see each
other's faces and Lucy saw Niccolo scowl.

'The *Inglese* do not observe our strict propriety,' he
began.

'Lucia is under my protection,' the Conte cut in. 'She
will be treated like my own daughter until she becomes
your wife, Nicco.' He smiled sardonically. 'Your rap-
tures will be increased by continence now.'

Banked fires to burn all the more fiercely when released. Lucy shivered silently. She knew well enough
why the Conte was forcing restraint upon his stepson.
He did not want the keenness of his desire to be
whetted before he was safely married to her. She was
only a pawn in the game he was playing and her feelings mattered to him not one jot, but to do him justice,
he considered she had a great deal to gain by this
alliance. Niccolo was not a pauper and had great ex-
pectations, besides being a personable young man. Any
sensible girl would jump at him and she would be a
fool not to appreciate her good fortune. Nevertheless
some compunction caused him to say when they
reached her door and he noticed her white face:

'You need not fear, Lucia, I will ensure that Niccolo
makes you a good husband.'

He could too, by virtue of holding the purse strings.

Any deviations on Niccolo's part would be countered by the threat of disinheritance.

'Thank you, *signore*,' Lucy returned. 'But I'm capable of managing my own life.'

A gleam of appreciation showed in his deep set eyes.

'I believe you are—you are a courageous woman, Lucia, you and Nicco should have fine children.'

He sighed, for it was part of his grievance against Caterina that she had failed to give him a son. After Carlotta's birth her doctor had told him it was unlikely she would bear more children. It was particularly hard, because his first wife, Niccolo's mother, had produced a male child before he had married her, but had been unable to present him with one.

Of this underlying frustration Lucy was of course unaware, and as he closed the door behind her her thoughts took a new direction. Children ... Niccolo's children. She had always hoped that one day she would meet a man whom she could love and they would have a family. She loved children, hence her choice of a profession, but looking after other people's could not compensate for not having any of her own. But if she gave Niccolo children she feared he might resent their foreign blood—true, he had told her the dark blood usually prevailed, and she would be the mother of a brood of little Sicilians, from whom he might try to alienate her, the fair-haired stranger, who was good enough to bed but not to wed. Then if he succeeded to the Conte's wealth would they not be exposed to the dangers which threatened Carlotta, and be unable to lead a normal childhood? Though for a moment she had wavered, for the thought of bearing Niccolo's children was very sweet, Lucy thrust it away from her.

There were too many hazards and too great a risk of heartbreak. Niccolo, being Sicilian, would adore his offspring, but that might cause him to further resent his wife because they were not wholly so; she knew his fierce national pride. She gave a long sigh as she crept beneath the covers of her cold bed. Her resolve had strengthened; she must leave Sicily.

Paolina brought Lucy coffee and rolls to her bedroom at a fairly early hour. The old master, she told her, wanted to start while the day was still cool. She looked with approval at the tumbled bed which showed no sign of having been shared by Niccolo. The virgin was still immaculate and now the Conte had come to take her away before her young master could violate her. Paolina held primitive views, she did not object to the women Niccolo sometimes brought to Valpena—a young man needed release for his natural urges—but they were girls who lived by their wits and in the English phrase were 'no better than they should be'. Lucy, she had recognised at once, was of a different sort and innocent. She still had a heart to break. Though she adored Niccolo, Paolina had disapproved of his behaviour towards Lucy and was glad she was leaving unscathed.

Watching her as she shot furtive glances about the room, seeking for any trace of Niccolo's presence, Lucia guessed her thoughts and flushed uncomfortably.

'You go with the Conte?' the woman asked in her heavily accented English. Lucy nodded.

'That is well,' Paolina said with satisfaction. 'Signor Martelli . . .' she shrugged her shoulders. ' 'E no good for such as you.'

Lucy thought ironically that her words were only too

true. Left alone, she drank the coffee but felt no appetite for the rolls. How different the situation would be if Niccolo really loved her! The Cinderella story come true, but in fairy stories such situations were in black and white. The heroes loved or hated, there were no complications of desire without love or divided loyalties, and the princes' intentions were always honourable. Lucy sighed. No use pondering upon unlikely might-have-beens. Even if Niccolo did love her, he would not want to marry a foreign nannie, were he free to make his own choice. She experienced a moment of rebellion, why not accept what had been thrust upon her? Take her moment of ecstasy and hang the consequences? She might come in time to love this beautiful island. But as quickly as it had been born the impulse died. Back in Syracuse Niccolo would come again under the Contessa's influence. That she would exert it to the full to recall her errant lover was a foregone conclusion. Lucy could imagine the yearning glances passing between the two while the Conte organised the preparations for her marriage. How he would gloat over Caterina's fury and despair ... and Niccolo? Would he be able to resist the advances of his former love? He probably would not even try to do so. There would be stolen meetings; Caterina too could be cunning. Niccolo would come to her on their wedding night expecting a substitute for her embraces, and how could she, a modest inexperienced English girl, compete with the volcanic passions of that sultry woman? She would be inadequate and he would be disappointed, secretly resenting her for forcing him into a false position. No, she could never endure such humiliation.

Lucy repacked her cases and was ready for the journey when she was summoned downstairs. The mountain showed only a plume of smoke over the smouldering crater. Its vast bulk dominated the countryside.

Beppo put her cases into the boot of the Conte's car, while the Conte himself greeted her warmly. He was all smiles, having obtained his way, and was savouring his revenge. He enquired if she had had any sleep, and promised her a long siesta when they had reached the villa to make up for her broken night. Lucy said it was worth being disturbed to have seen the volcano in action. They were standing outside the house in the warm sunshine, waiting to take leave of their host, for Niccolo was that, and Lucy was on edge for his appearance. If she could have followed her inclination, she would have driven off without saying goodbye. He came out, immaculately shaved, wearing a fawn linen shirt and brown trousers. He apologised for keeping them waiting, saying he had overslept, an excuse that incensed Lucy. While she had been restless and troubled, he apparently had enjoyed unbroken slumber, but had she looked at him, which she did not, she would have noticed dark marks beneath his eyes, which hinted at strain. His manner was polite and aloof. He would be coming to Syracuse later in the day, he told them, and he hoped Carlotta would be home by then. He cocked a questioning eyebrow at the Conte.

'I myself will bring her back,' the Conte told him, 'And of course Lucia will no longer act as her nannie.'

'Oh, but I'd like ...' Lucy began anxiously, but he cut her short.

'You may play with her if you desire, but naturally

as the *fidanzata* of my heir, you will be treated as an
honoured guest, not a dependent.'

'So when I arrive I shall find you in the *salotto*, not
the nursery,' Niccolo said pointedly, a little teasing
smile curving his lips. 'Sewing your wedding clothes,
perhaps.'

'And chaperoned by my wife,' the Conte added with
a gleam in his eyes.

Lucy quailed at the prospect.

'I've no money for a trousseau,' she said bluntly.

'*Non importa*, my wife will obtain all that is necessary,' the Conte told her. An inimical glance passed
between the two men. The Conte was intending to
enjoy every moment of his bitter triumph; he meant to
turn the screw so that every twist should cause the
supposed lovers a pang, but the one who would suffer
most was the unoffending girl who stood pale and collected between them.

'Damn you!' Niccolo burst out with a sudden blaze of
passion. 'You cannot do this to Lucy! Why not set her
up in a hotel?'

So he did understand her feelings and had some consideration for them. Lucy gave him a grateful look.

'Most unsuitable,' the Conte drawled. 'She must have
a chaperone, and the obvious person is my wife.'

Lucy noticed he referred to Caterina as his wife
upon every occasion and with heavy emphasis. 'You
may visit her every day,' the older man went on with
the air of one bestowing a great favour, 'but only in
my wife's presence, of course.'

Niccolo clenched his hands, obviously restraining a
further outburst. Lucy was sorry for him; though her
position was bad enough, his was worse. She wondered

if Caterina would not solve all their problems by sticking a stiletto into either herself or Niccolo. She was quite capable of doing so.

'May I speak to Lucy alone?' Niccolo asked.

'Certainly not. You will not be alone with her again until your wedding night,' the Conte decreed. 'Though Lucia is a foreigner, your courtship will be conducted according to the best Sicilian traditions.' He turned to Lucy. 'Come, my dear, bid your *fidanzato* farewell and let us be on our way.'

Niccolo took a step towards her and for a moment Lucy thought he was going to ignore his stepfather's presence and embrace her. His eyes were smouldering and he was evidently very angry at the Conte's high-handed assumption of command. But he checked himself, and lifting her hand touched it with his lips.

'*Arrivederci, amore mia*,' he said lightly.

'Goodbye, Nicco,' Lucy responded. Her eyes travelled over his lithe graceful figure, his handsome face with wistful longing. She did not mean to see him again. Quick to interpret her moods, he exclaimed:

'Do not speak as if we were parting for ever! I shall see you again in a few hours.'

Under the Contessa's watchful eyes? Lucy shook her head slightly. 'Perhaps.'

'There is no doubt about it,' the Conte declared jovially. 'What do you think is going to happen, Lucia? I am a careful driver and if you have survived Nicco's impetuosity on the roads, you will survive my caution.'

'I'm sure I shall,' Lucy said gravely, thinking an accident would solve all her difficulties. She did not greatly care what happened to her and it would save her the wrench of finally tearing herself away from

Niccolo. For standing there in the early morning sunshine with the prospect of parting ahead of her, she
knew that he would leave an indelible mark upon her
heart. Whatever he was, whatever he had done. No
other man would ever affect her as he did. She supposed it must be love ... could one love a man who
appeared to be something of a reprobate? But funda-
mentally she was aware that that was nothing to do
with it. Niccolo was Niccolo, she had never met anyone
like him before, and she never would again. When she
left Sicily, she would leave her heart behind her.

'Come along, my dear,' the Conte said impatiently,
and taking her arm, led her towards his car. '*Ciao*,
Nicco,' he threw carelessly over his shoulder.

He helped her ceremoniously into the passenger seat,
and closed the door. Lucy looked out of the window
towards the house, but Niccolo had already gone inside. The Conte took his seat beside her and drove
carefully down the rough road towards the smoother
highway. Lucy looked back and glimpsed through
the rear window the red roof of Niccolo's house amidst
its trees and bushes, with the frowning bulk of the
mountain behind it with its ominous plume of smoke.
Then a bend in the road cut it off from her sight and
they were travelling through acres of vineyards.

'It is a curious fact,' the Conte remarked conver-
sationally, 'that there are very few villages in Sicily.
The Siciliano hates being isolated, he prefers to travel
a long way to work and live in a town ...' He went on
relating the peculiarities of his countrymen, which he
expected would soon be hers. Lucy barely listened; her
mind was occupied with the reception she would get
at the Villa di Santa Croce. She must see the Contessa

alone as soon as possible—there would probably be no
difficulty about that—and enlist her help to get out of
the country. But the prospect filled her with intense de-
pression.

When they reached the Villa the early morning cool
had given place to the glaring heat of a Mediterranean
day. At the Conte's imperious ringing of the front door
bell, Franco opened to them and showed a momentary
surprise at the sight of Lucy, which quickly changed
to impassivity. The Conte told him to leave the car
where it was, as he would be using it later, and asked
if the Contessa had come downstairs. The man replied
that Madonna was in the *salotto*.

'*Bene.*' The Conte turned to Lucy. 'We will hasten to
tell her our good news.' There was an anticipatory
glitter in his eyes.

'*Signore*,' Lucy pleaded, 'please may I be excused? I
will see her later, of course, but I'm tired . . .'

'You will see her now,' the Conte informed her implacably. His arm closed over her arm in a vicelike
grip, and thus joined, they entered the *salotto*.

The Contessa was not reclining on the settee but
sitting at her davenport, a charming period piece, and
was writing busily. She wore a dark silk dress, her
luxuriant hair drawn back and knotted in her nape.
Long gold ear-rings hung from her ears. She looked up
in surprise at their entry, and Lucy had an intuition
that she was writing to Niccolo, for one plump hand
spread itself over the paper.

'Alfonso! *Cosa c'e?*' Her eyes went to Lucy. '*Dio mio*,
that *ragazza* again!'

Her husband released Lucy's arm and crossing to
the writing desk, tweaked the half-covered sheet from

under her hand. He ran his eye over it, uttered an exclamation of disgust and tore it into shreds. The Contessa leaned back in her chair and loosed a flood of invective at him, of which he took no notice. She pointed to Lucy and was evidently including her in her tirade, for the Conte laughed triumphantly, then said impatiently:

'*Basta*, prepare yourself for some good news. Lucia and Nicco are betrothed.' He spoke in English for Lucy's benefit. The Contessa went red, then white.

'It is not possible,' she said flatly. 'I do not believe it.'

'It is perfectly true. I have brought Lucia from Valpena where Nicco took her after you turned her out. So you have only yourself to blame, since the poor girl had nowhere to go. But since she spent the night there, she is hopelessly compromised and Nicco is prepared to do the right thing and make an honest woman of her.'

Caterina opened and closed her mouth like a gasping fish. She tried to rise, then fell back in her chair, and Lucy started forward, fearing she was about to have a stroke. Evidently the Conte thought so too, and that was no part of his scheming. He raised her from her chair and supported her to the settee.

'Lie down, my love—I see I have broken the news too abruptly, though you, with your woman's instinct must have noticed those two were drawn to each other. Perhaps a glass of wine would revive you. Lucia sit down, I am sure you would like some refreshment after the drive.'

He rang the bell for service and fussed over his wife, all seeming solicitude, arranging a cushion behind her head. Lucy sat down in a chair at a distance from them, feeling her legs would not support her. The Conte's merciless taunts shocked her. The scene was totally unreal, like a bad melodrama. Caterina was deathly pale, her eyes huge and full of venom as they rested upon her. The Conte gave his orders to the servant who had come in answer to his summons. As the man withdrew they watched his exit from the room as if he were of supreme importance, nor did they speak until he re-entered with his tray of glasses and bottles. Alfonso proceeded to play the courteous host. He knew his wife's preference, he said, she liked red wine, but Lucy, he was sure, would prefer white. He filled the wine glasses and handed them to their recipients. As Lucy took hers, Caterina snapped:

'I wish it were poison, you traitress!'

'I daresay you do,' the Conte returned urbanely. 'But Lucia is not a traitress, only a young girl deeply in love.' He shot her a meaning glance. 'You cannot blame her for that—Nicco is, as you know all too well, the embodiment of a maiden's dream. Fortunately for her, he returns her passion.' He took a sip of his wine. 'Her freshness and innocence appeal to a taste sated by more mature charms. We would be cruel to seek to part them, so I have given them my blessing, and will not you drink to their happiness?'

He had seated himself beside her on the settee, and the Contessa threw the contents of her glass full in his mocking face. The red wine ran down his cheeks like spilled blood, and he wiped it away imperturbably. Only for a second had his face contorted with fury, and instantly became impassive again.

'You will pay for that,' he said pleasantly, 'and your conduct is more like that of a peasant girl than a lady of quality. Are you not ashamed to show your lack of control in front of Lucia?'

He stood up, refilled his glass and drained it. 'I wish you to discuss with Lucia the clothes she will need as befits Nicco's bride. Meanwhile, after I have changed my shirt,' he glanced down at its stained front, 'I will go to bring Carlotta home. I will give orders that the best guest room is prepared for Lucia.'

Lucy rose quickly to her feet. The scene she had witnessed had appalled her. As an example of Sicilian vindictiveness it was an object lesson; did Nicco also possess that streak of cruelty? She was sorry for the Contessa, but she shrank from being left alone with her after what had been said.

'Please, *signore* ...' she began, her eyes wide with appeal.

'You will remain here,' he commanded brutally. 'My wife, I am sure, has a great deal to say to you.'

So she was not to be spared either. In spite of all his pretended consideration, he owed her a grudge for becoming involved with Niccolo; though she suited his purpose, she was not really the wife he would have chosen for his heir. About to protest further, she recollected that now was her opportunity to appeal to Caterina for help, so she sat down obediently.

The Conte looked at her doubtfully; he had seen the flash of rebellion in her eyes.

'One small matter before I leave—would you hand me your passport?'

So he did not trust her entirely. Summoning all her resolution, Lucy gave him a bright smile. 'It's in one of my cases,' she told him, though actually it was in her handbag. 'It'll take time to find it and I'm sure you don't want to be delayed. Surely you don't imagine I'd dream of running away after pledging myself to Nicco?'

He seemed satisfied and went out of the room. Lucy was left to face the enraged Contessa.

CHAPTER SEVEN

No two women could have presented a greater contrast than the Sicilian Contessa and the English nannie— Caterina in her rich silk dress, all opulent curves, her great black eyes full of fire and fury, her fingers restlessly toying with her ear-rings and necklace, and Lucy, slim as a reed in her simple white dress, her grey gaze steady and watchful, and her hands demurely folded in her lap. She was wondering how to make her request.

The other woman made no attempt to restrain herself. As soon as the door closed behind the Conte she burst out savagely:

'So, you have got what you wanted. Do you think I did not know what was behind those expeditions with Nicco? His visits to the nursery? Carlotta indeed—it was not she he went to see, but I am surprised he allowed himself to be caught by your obvious guile— you, a penniless English adventuress, worming your way into my household with your sly underhand ways! First you impose upon my husband, and then Niccolo...' She changed into virulent Italian, becoming more and more excited as she poured out abuse, raising herself on the settee like a coiled snake, and her eyes glowed red with rage. Lucy was sure that if she had had a weapon handy she would have used it. When at length she had to pause for breath, Lucy said quietly:

'Please don't distress yourself, *signora*. I've no intention of marrying Signor Martelli.'

The Contessa stared unbelievingly at the girl.

'But that is what you have worked and schemed to bring about!'

Lucy shook her head. 'I never dreamed of it. I'm sure Signor Martelli's actions were motivated entirely by his affection for Carlotta. He is fond of her, you know.' Caterina snorted. 'Oh, but he is. I'll admit that his manner towards me was more familiar than it should have been, but I thought that was his approach to any good-looking girl, not being used to Italian men.' The Contessa's eyes narrowed and she seemed about to speak, but Lucy went serenely on.

'You turned me out, madam, after wrongly accusing me.' Her eyes became reproachful. 'I'd nowhere to go and very little money, so when Signor Martelli offered to help me I accepted his aid. I had meant to go to the British Consulate in Palermo, but he warned me you might have alerted the police there—I didn't know then that your daughter had not been kidnapped.'

'So he took you to his love nest at Valpena,' the Contessa sneered. 'I can guess the rest.'

'Then you haven't much faith in his fidelity,' Lucy countered, and Caterina looked disconcerted. Lucy wondered if she were as sure of Niccolo's devotion as she pretended to be, but her next words dispelled the fleeting doubt.

'He is young and impressionable, your blonde colouring is attractive to southern men. But I will swear he only wanted a night's diversion and no thought of a permanent union was in his mind. His lasting allegiance is to me.'

'I don't question it,' Lucy told her, stifling the pain this statement evoked. She had never doubted that Caterina was Niccolo's real love. She herself had been, as the Contessa said, merely a companion for a night's entertainment. Continual frustration needed an outlet, and Niccolo was sufficiently attracted by her to accept her as a temporary assuagement. She had never supposed she meant anything more to him. She went on steadily: 'Your husband discovered where I was and ...' she faltered as her heartbeat quickened recalling Niccolo's lovemaking. 'He ... er ... intervened. For reasons of his own which perhaps you can understand.' She looked directly into the opaque black eyes and saw the Contessa wince. 'He insists we should marry.'

'And Nicco agreed?'

Lucy dropped her eyes and pulled aimlessly at her skirt. 'Faced with the loss of his inheritance if he didn't comply, he did.'

'Ah!' Caterina drew a long breath and some of the tension went out of her attitude. 'That I can understand. But you?'

'I was in a difficult position, *signora*,' Lucy pleaded. 'It seemed best to pretend to agree.'

'And to be brought here to flaunt your triumph in my face?' Caterina cried shrilly, 'with a command to order your bride clothes?'

'Which you need not do, *signora*, if you will help me to return to England.'

Astonishment followed by disbelief flitted across the Contessa's face, but her next question came as a surprise to Lucy.

'What have you got against Nicco?'

'Why, nothing, *signora*!' Lucy exclaimed. 'But such

a marriage would be entirely unsuitable, with no chance of happiness for either of us. Besides, he belongs to you.'

For the first time since she had known her, Lucy saw Caterina smile. It lightened the heaviness of her face and lent her a fleeting charm. Thus Niccolo must often see her, she thought sadly, a wholly different person from the sullen aspect she usually presented in her company.

'I had no idea you had so much good sense, *signorina*,' she said approvingly. 'The door behind you is not locked. If you are sincere ... go.'

Lucy did not move. 'Before I go I require a reference from you as to my capabilities,' she said calmly. 'Also Franco may have orders to stop me, and some salary is due to me. I haven't enough cash for the flight to England.'

The Contessa looked at her oddly, then she laughed. Her laughter was deep and throaty. 'You certainly have . what you say ... your head screwed on firmly.' She walked across to the writing desk, raised the lid and extracted a thick wad of notes. 'That should cover your requirements. The reference you shall have, though I perjure myself to give it. Franco has probably gone with my husband, but I will provide transport for you to the airport.'

Lucy took the notes and put them in her handbag while the Contessa sat down and scribbled some words on a sheet of headed paper.

'I have told whom it may concern that you fulfilled your duties *with regard to my daughter* satisfactorily,' she said as she signed her name with a flourish. 'We will hope there are no young men about the house in your next post.' She rang the bell beside her. 'There take it.'

Lucy added the paper to the notes in her bag.

'Thank you, *signora*.'

A servant entered the room.

'Send Giuseppe to me,' his mistress commanded, and he withdrew.

The Contessa said to Lucy: 'You shall have my own car and my personal bodyguard to take you to the airport, but you will not fly from Catania. That is where my husband might look for you. I shall tell him you are going from there to England, after borrowing your fare from me, being as unwilling as I am sure Signor Martelli is to contract this marriage. He may not listen to me, and will try to catch you. We must guard against that.'

'You mean I could go from Palermo?'

'Yes, but not until tonight. The Conte might make enquiries there, but by nightfall he will be convinced you have evaded him. Meanwhile Giuseppe will drive you round the Island, for of course you cannot stay here. They call it the Golden Ribbon route, you have heard of it perhaps. It will be an *interesting* trip.' She smiled maliciously. 'Ah, Giuseppe!'

The man who came in fumbling with his chauffeur's cap was not prepossessing. Small eyes stared furtively from under beetling eyebrows. He was short and stocky with a thatch of uncombed hair and a day's growth of beard.

'Giuseppe has no English,' the Contessa told her. She addressed the man at some length in the dialect, at the end of which, he grinned showing broken teeth.

'He is not beautiful,' she said to Lucy in English,

'but he is devoted to me and will carry out my orders implicitly.' She gave Lucy a penetrating look. 'You really mean to go? You will not try to sneak back to Signor Martelli?'

'Believe me, *signora*,' Lucy said earnestly, 'that is the last thing I want to do.' And she felt her heart contract; suddenly she wanted Niccolo very badly. She did not like the look of her proffered escort and if she had not been certain that the Contessa was dying to get rid of her, she would not have trusted her. The Conte was definitely an enemy, but Niccolo, she felt sure, would have been decent enough to help her on her way once he understood her reluctance to stay.

The Contessa repeated her instructions to her chauffeur, and he asked one or two questions which she answered placatingly. There was a feverish glitter in her eyes, and Lucy wondered whether where Niccolo was concerned if she were quite sane.

Giuseppe went out carrying Lucy's cases, and Caterina said he would meet them with the car at the garden entrance. Franco had gone with the Conte, and the other well trained servants were invisible. Caterina walked with her through the garden and outside the gate was parked the limousine which was reserved for her private use. It was a heavy old-fashioned vehicle, but its interior was roomy and comfortable. Lucy was ushered into the back seat, and the Contessa stood watching them drive off with such a malignant expression that Lucy turned cold. She was thankful to see the last of Caterina di Santa Croce.

Though Sicily is not a very big island Lucy knew that her journey would take a long time, as they were following a circuitous route, and the Contessa had in-

sisted she should not appear in Palermo until dusk.
As they had left Syracuse at midday, Giuseppe did not
hurry, knowing he had six or seven hours in which to
do the trip. Lucy supposed the precaution was necessary. If the Conte did go on to Palermo in search of her
he would travel by the northern route, never dreaming
she had gone south.

Giuseppe stopped en route to bring her refreshment,
sandwiches and orange juice. She refused the food but
was glad of the drink. They had stopped at a small
albergo on the fringe of a town. Anticipating another
need, he indicated a wooden shack which contained a
hole in the ground, the usual primitive convenience in
out-of-the-way places. Lucy thought he might have
found something better for her; she would not have
been conspicuous amid the tourists. He drove in his
shirt sleeves, abandoning his jacket in the heat, and his
arms were covered with black hair. Lucy was surprised
any employee of the Contessa's should be so uncouth,
but no doubt he smartened himself up when driving
his mistress. He saw no necessity to stand on ceremony
with an ex-nannie. As they travelled further and further west, she began to feel uneasy. Giuseppe looked
capable of any villainy and she had a good deal of
money in her bag. In the bright sunlight, with plenty
of people about, there was no cause for alarm, but
the final stage of the journey would be in the dark
through country quite unknown to her, but surely
Caterina's personal chauffeur would be an honest man?
If she could have communicated with him, she would
have asked him to take a shorter route, so as to arrive
sooner, for surely by now the Conte would be convinced that she had left the country, but he indicated

that he could not understand anything she said, and
possibly there was no short cut, for the interior of the
country was barren and mountainous, given over to
sheep and corn-growing and sparsely populated.

They had passed through Sciacco, a town on a hill
where the close-packed houses descended to sandy
beaches, when Lucy noticed the white sports car following them. Her mouth became dry and her heart
beat faster—for that car was familiar. It was not near
enough to read the number plate, and Italian ones
have smaller figures than English ones, but it looked
like Niccolo's, though why he should want to follow
her she could not conceive. Caterina would have found
an opportunity to tell him how neatly she had disposed
of his unwanted *fidanzata* and he would be congratu-
lating himself upon being free of her, unless the Conte
was with him. But the car appeared to have only one
occupant, a dark-haired man, though she could not
distinguish his features. Giuseppe, it seemed, had
recognised the car, for he increased his speed, and was
obviously trying to shake it off. He took fearful risks,
but still the white car pursued them. Lucy was completely mystified. If it were Niccolo trailing them,
though that seemed inexplicable, why was Giuseppe
so anxious to evade him? Surely the sensible thing to
do would be to stop and ask him what he wanted. She
did not believe he would want to stop her from reaching Palermo, but something unexpected might have
happened that he thought they ought to know, so why
this mad chase? Was it excess of zeal on Giuseppe's
part? She did not want to encounter Niccolo, but
neither did she want to be killed in an accident.
Though she had felt she did not much care what be-

came of her it was not a pleasant way to end.

She leaned over the back of the front seat, shouting, *'Fermi!* Stop—*pericolo!'* hoping one word might be familiar to her driver, but the man took no notice, merely shaking his head as if a fly were buzzing in his ears, and the car careered on.

A sharp bend in the road took them momentarily out of sight of their pursuer. There was a dirt track leading off one side of it, lined with trees and undergrowth, and with a swerve that threw Lucy across the car, Giuseppe took it. It twisted and turned through groves of lemon trees, and the car bumped along its rutted surface. Then, rounding a bend, they were brought to a halt. Coming towards them was one of the painted carts characteristic of Sicily, drawn by a gaily caparisoned horse, with a plume on its head and another rising from its saddle. The cart, not only its body but the wheels, spokes and shafts, was covered with ornate patterns in bright colours. A whole family in their gala clothes were riding in it, evidently on the way to some *festa.* One of the them was strumming on a guitar. At any other time Lucy would have been delighted to see it, but now it was a barrier to their progress. Giuseppe evidently hoped Niccolo would have missed the turning, but if the white car was behind them they were trapped.

A violent altercation took place, the driver of the cart insisting that Giuseppe should reverse, while he was urging the lighter vehicle should back into the hedge to give him passage. Since the hedge was composed mainly of prickly pear and there was a ditch the driver's reluctance was understandable. Finally, exasperated and anxious to make his getaway from the

pursuer on the road, Giuseppe jumped out of the car
and going to the horse seized its bridle, forcing it to
back. At the same moment the bonnet of the white car
appeared round the bend. Lucy could never have explained the impulse which prompted her next action.
Reason, if she had had time to reason, would have indicated that she should avoid Niccolo. Why he had
come after her was a puzzle, but the object of her flight
was to escape him, and the position his stepfather had
put them in. Perhaps instinct warned her that
Giuseppe was untrustworthy, and the brutal way he
was handing the horse revolted her. She was out of the
car in a flash and racing towards the one behind it. It
had halted within a few yards of the limousine, and
its engine was still running. Niccolo, for it was Niccolo,
opened the door as he saw her coming, and as she
reached it, thrust out a hand to pull her into it. With
his other hand on the wheel he started to reverse.

'Shut the door,' he said through clenched teeth as
she tumbled into the passenger seat, and as she obeyed
him she saw that Giuseppe had re-entered the limousine, and the heavy vehicle was backing towards them.

It was only about a quarter of a mile on to the road,
but it seemed like a hundred as the bulk of the limousine bore down upon them. Both cars were reversing,
but the lane sloped downwards, so the heavier vehicle
seemed to be gaining. Niccolo's face was set, and sweat
gathered on his upper lip as he concentrated upon
keeping the sports car on the track. To stall or stick
would mean an instant collision. Lucy was flung about
in her seat as the car lurched and bumped and she
grasped at the seat belt.

'Put it on,' Niccolo ordered, and she fumbled with

the fastening, and finally secured it. She realised that to be thrown against Niccolo might mean disaster.

'Has he gone mad?' she gasped. 'He'll run into us!'

Niccolo did not answer, and swore as the back wheels sank in a rut, but the game little car pulled out of it, and they continued their erratic course. Lucy knew that if the limousine caught them, the light sports car would be completely shattered, but Giuseppe in front of the other car might escape. That significant fact stuck in her mind with all its sinister implication, though it was absurd to think Giuseppe would dare to injure Niccolo, for the Contessa would never forgive him for that.

At last the back wheels of the sports car touched the metalled surface of the main road. Niccolo spun it round and they were away. He laughed triumphantly, for the danger had exhilarated him, his black eyes were sparkling and his teeth gleamed. He was vibrant with energy and devastatingly attractive.

'He cannot catch us now. This car is faster than that old hearse.'

Lucy shivered at the rather unfortunate simile, and her brow wrinkled in perplexity.

'But, Nicco, I don't understand—why did he act like that?'

'I will explain when we have shaken him off. Watch the road behind us, will you, I need all my concentration to keep us going.'

She noticed he had turned westward away from Syracuse; so he did not intend to take her back, he might even be going to Palermo.

They raced along the highway, weaving in and out between cars and buses, cutting in shamefully. They

flashed through coastal towns at a speed which Lucy
felt sure must be illegal, but Italians have no respect
for traffic rules, and still the black shadow followed
them. They had numerous near misses, but Niccolo
was a superb driver and Lucy caught something of his
excitement; she was past being afraid, and she was
thrilled and happy to be by his side during that wild
drive. Almost she could wish it would end there, then
she would never have to part from him again or face
any more problems. They would be united in death as
they never could be in life. The westering sun turned
the road molten ahead of them, a veritable golden
ribbon. A pathway to paradise.

There was a loud explosion and Lucy saw the pursuing car slew to the side of the road.

'A burst tire,' Niccolo said with satisfaction. 'He will
give up now.' He slackened speed.

Lucy was completely fogged as to why Giuseppe had
pursued them at all. Surely his responsibility for her
had ended when she had chosen to enter Niccolo's car,
but she was very glad to have disposed of her grim
escort. They had passed Marsala on Cape Boeo and
were running up the west coast of Sicily towards
Trapani through a flat alluvial plain bordering the sea.
It was dotted with windmills and, near the coast, saltpans. Inland there were fields starred with flowers—
gladioli, snapdragons, cyclamen and small blue irises.
In the distance was the outline of hills and out at sea
the rocky shapes of the Aegadian Islands swimming in
a sea of gold as the sun sank towards the horizon.

Tired after the heat and ordeals of the day, Lucy was
in a state of drowsy euphoria. Nothing seemed real, perhaps she was dreaming? Maybe the limousine had run

into them after all, and she had been transported to paradise, the impact having been too sudden for her to have any recollection of it. The scenery was beautiful enough to be the Elysian Fields. Niccolo had not spoken again, and surely his presence beside her was something of a miracle. She had believed him to be in Syracuse, making his peace with Caterina for his apparent desertion. He was driving slowly now, at least his pace seemed so after what had gone before, and kept his eyes on the road ahead, as remote as an archangel. But there was nothing ethereal about him, and when as she moved in her seat her thigh brushed his, it felt very solid. No, she had not passed to a better world, she was still in this one with further tribulations ahead of her, but for the moment all was peace.

'We are coming into Trapani.' Niccolo broke the spell which had enwrapped her, and his voice sounded very ordinary as if they were upon a normal excursion. 'I know a quiet hotel run by nice people where we can rest and eat. You need to relax after that experience.'

'So we're not going back to Syracuse?'

'We are travelling in the opposite direction.' He flashed a quick look at her. 'Do you want to return there?'

'Good lord, no!' she exclaimed vehemently. 'I want to get to Palermo and take a flight home.'

'So you are running out on me?'

'Not you especially, but I felt my position was intolerable.'

'I am sorry to hear that.'

'Oh, don't pretend,' she said wearily. 'You can't have wanted me to stay.' She roused herself from the inertia which bound her. 'I don't understand what all this is about. Was Giuseppe annoyed because I got into your car? I don't know what made me do it. The Contessa lent me her own car and her chauffeur...'

'That thug!' he interjected.

'Well, I was surprised he looked so disreputable, but she gave him his orders herself. He was to take me to Palermo...'

'You would not have arrived there.'

Lucy failed to take in the significance of his words. She was remembering that all her possessions were in her cases in the other car, and it did not look as if she would ever see them again.

'I've lost my luggage, and it's all your fault,' she complained. 'Why on earth did you have to come zooming after me?'

'Because you had foolishly put your trust in the wrong people, *cara*.'

She sighed despairingly. 'It seems I can't trust anybody on this island.' It would appear she was as far away as ever from getting away from it, and she was suspicious of Niccolo's intentions. Thanks to her own rash action she had put herself completely in his power, and she did not feel strong enough to face another emotional scene with him.

'At least you had the good sense to come to me,' he told her—a remark the situation did not seem to warrant.

'I'm just wondering about that,' she said, her head drooping. There would be no Conte to arrive to intervene this time.

Niccolo noticed her exhaustion.

'We are nearly there,' he said kindly, as the houses

along the route began to thicken. '*Poverina*, you are worn out.'

'I am,' she admitted, heartened by the sympathetic note in his voice. Perhaps he could be persuaded to help her on her way. After all, he had not wanted to become engaged to her and once she had gone he would be free. For some reason he had not approved of Giuseppe, but he must know the Contessa was as anxious to get her out of the country as she was to go.

Trapani, from Drepanon meaning scythe, was built on a curved peninsula, and in Greek times had been an important port and it was still a busy one. It was composed of tall ochre-coloured houses built along the waterline of the northern arm of the shore; to the south the aspect was bleak, with docks, mud banks and salt marshes. Behind it was the rocky eminence on the crest of which was the secluded town of Erice. Niccolo drove down a narrow winding street along the northern isthmus, and pulled up in front of a tall hotel, the back of which was towards the sea.

In silence he helped her out of the car, stiff and weary with fatigue, and in silence she followed him into the vestibule, standing to one side while he conferred with the receptionist, who greeted him as an old friend. The place seemed thronged with tourists in transit, sun tanned and full of zest. Lucy watched them with lacklustre eyes, her spirits sunk to zero by this interruption in her journey. True, she did need food and rest, she had not eaten all day, but surely they could have found both in Palermo, which could not be very far away.

A smiling chambermaid appeared and beckoned to her to follow her. She showed Lucy into a ground floor suite with a view of the sea. Being air-conditioned it was quiet and cool. There was a sitting room, bedroom and bathroom, simply furnished but comfortable. Lucy went into the bathroom and washed her face and hands, sighing for her lost cases. She would have liked to be able to change, but she possessed nothing except what she stood up in. She went back into the sitting room, sat down on a settee, putting her feet up, and dully watched the setting sun over the sea.

The proximity of the bedroom worried her. Why had it been necessary to engage a whole suite? Was Niccolo contemplating a repetition of Valpena? He meant to have his way with her before sending her back to England. Thus he would satisfy his desire before disposing of an unwanted bride. She could not believe he would be quite such a heel, though she could think of no other explanation for his actions. She had been perfectly crazy to leave the security of the limousine to enter his sports car. Now the excitement of the chase and the euphoria which had followed it had died down, she realised she had only herself to blame for her impulsive folly.

She was half asleep when a knock on the door aroused her. A waiter entered with a dinner trolley and after him came Niccolo carrying a new suitcase.

'Ah, food,' he exclaimed cheerfully. 'You must be starving.'

'I'm not hungry.'

'Nonsense, you must eat.'

The waiter placed a low table in front of her and laid out his wares upon it—smoked ham, salad, bread rolls, butter, cheese and fruit, and what was most welcome a big glass jug of fresh orange juice with ice clinking in it. He went away and Niccolo drew up a chair opposite to Lucy and began to serve her.

'I bought you a few necessities,' he told her, indicating the suitcase, 'since your luggage is lost.'

'But, Nicco, I can't stay here,' she cried in alarm.

'I don't intend that you shall, but it is unlikely that you can get on a flight tonight, so I propose to take you up to Erice, that is that town on top of the mountain. I have friends there who will make you very welcome, until we can book a seat for you. The summer season is starting and you might have to wait a day or two. You will be quite safe with them.'

'Safe?' she echoed, wrinkling her brows. 'Why the cloak and dagger touch? The Contessa wants to be rid of me.'

'She certainly does, but finally and for ever. Giuseppe was instructed to cause an accident in some remote spot, preferably after dark, and you can be quite sure you would not have been allowed to survive it.'

Lucy stared at him in horror. 'Then ... then when he backed the car down the lane he was deliberately trying to ram us?'

'That was the idea. He, being in the front of the heavier car, would probably not have been hurt, but as for us ...' He shrugged his shoulders and helped himself to salad.

'But he knew you were in the sports car—the Contessa couldn't have wanted you to be harmed.'

Niccolo smiled sardonically. 'Giuseppe was unaware that I was ... er ... specially favoured,' he drawled. 'He only saw me as an obstruction to carrying out his orders.'

Lucy shuddered, feeling sick. 'How can you be so

calm about it?' she cried. 'It was dreadful!'

'There now, I have put you off your food,' Niccolo said contritely. 'But I thought I had better tell you what you were up against.' He put his hand over her's reassuringly. 'You are safe now, and you can put it out of your mind.'

'But, Nicco, this is supposed to be a civilised country, and the Contessa is a great lady.'

Niccolo withdrew his hand and started to eat.

'This is excellent ham,' he observed. 'Do try it.' He glanced at her quizzically. 'Under the veneer Caterina is as primitive as any savage. She is ruled by her emotions, love or hate, and regarding you and me she is almost paranoid. You must remember this is a country where strong passions lie close to the surface ready to erupt upon provocation. Ever heard of the Mafia?'

'Of course, but somehow one doesn't think of that sort of thing in connection with ordinary people ... the people one knows.'

'The Santa Croces are not ordinary people, and you do not know them at all.'

'I'm learning.' Lucy recalled the Conte's snide remarks. Caterina had had provocation.

And Niccolo was a connection of the family and probably equally capable of violent deeds, but on a grander scale. She could not conceive that he would stoop to bumping off inconvenient nannies, but the same leashed force was simmering inside him. Over-civilised herself, she had to admit it was part of his fascination for her; he was so different from the superficial youths she had known at home.

'How did you find out where I'd gone?' she asked, pushing at the food before her with her fork.

'Oh, Caterina told me. She seemed to think I would applaud her ingenuity. I had to use a little guile, pretend to play along with her to get the details. Then I came after you as fast as I could. You were a little idiot, Lucy, you played right into her hands.'

'But it didn't occur to me ... I never dreamed...'

'That she would go so far? No, I suppose it would not. But Papa should not have left you with her. It was like putting a lamb into a tiger's cage.'

His metaphor did not please Lucy, for sheep are silly animals, and she had stood up to the Contessa as well as she could. The bargain she had made with her had been to benefit him as much as herself, and where she had gone wrong was to not fully appreciate the intensity of the other woman's jealous hate. Caterina had been determined to ensure there could be no future meetings between Lucy and Niccolo by the most drastic means she could devise.

Lucy said anxiously: 'Will Giuseppe follow us here when he's changed his tire?'

'I doubt it.' Niccolo seemed indifferent to both past and future danger. 'He will not know where we have gone.' He lifted his head arrogantly. 'Now I am on my guard he will realise he will not get another chance to do his dirty work.'

Lucy was not wholly reassured; they were still some way from Palermo and the man's ill-favoured visage haunted her.

'Shouldn't you go to the police?' she suggested.

'What for? Do you think I cannot deal with this amateur assassin? This is a family matter, you would not want the whole story made public?'

'Oh, no, of course not,' Lucy hastily agreed.

'There is no need to be nervous, but just as a precaution, I am taking you to Erice. No one would dream of looking for you there, so you can sleep in peace. You look as though you need a good night's rest.'

In other words I'm looking a hag, Lucy thought. She did not at all want to meet Niccolo's friends, and she supposed they did exist; Erice, she had been told, was a somewhat isolated place being on top of a mountain. But Niccolo did not look at all amorous, and travel-stained and anxious, she could not appear glamorous. His manner towards her now was more like that of a kindly elder brother; he too would need a rest after that last mad race, though he appeared none the worse for his ordeal. She deduced from what she had been told that if Giuseppe had caught up with them he would have engineered a collision. She marvelled at Niccolo's sangfroid. He sat there, enjoying his meal as if it were the aftermath of a pleasure trip, and he looked as fresh and spruce as he had that morning at Valpena, when she had believed she had said goodbye to him for the last time. She could never have foreseen that before nightfall they would be alone together on the most westerly point of the island.

'I ... I suppose I owe you my life,' she said shyly, for though true, it seemed a melodramatic thing to say. Only now was she beginning to appreciate the magnitude of her indebtedness to him. But for his intervention she would be driving towards Palermo and her doom.

He waved his hand impatiently.

'Forget it.'

'Oh, but I can't ... ever. You've been wonderful, Nicco. I ... I don't know how to express my gratitude.'

His glance flashed up to her flushed face, with a glint in his eyes.

'Don't you?' he asked softly.

Involuntarily Lucy's glance went towards the bedroom door. So she could not be looking so unappetising after all! When she had entered the suite, she had been apprehensive of his intentions; now she had provoked the situation she had feared. She might have known how he would interpret her words. But she would not draw back, she owed him too much. She became even paler, and her eyes dropped to her plate, as she said faintly:

'I ... I'll do anything you want, Nicco, to show my gratitude.' Then as he said nothing, and she thought she had not made her meaning clear, she added: 'I'll sleep with you, if you like.'

CHAPTER EIGHT

THE last rays from the setting sun shone in at the window, gilding Lucy's hair, but that was the only colour about her; even her lips were pale. She looked like an alabaster image, her eyes veiled by her long lashes as she looked down upon her hands clasped upon the table. It was very quiet, no sound reaching them from the rest of the hotel, the guests being at dinner.

Niccolo was as silent and still as she was, only his black eyes moving as he studied her intently from top to toe. Lucy was waiting for his reaction, her strung nerves apparent in her tense attitude. She was expecting a burst of passion, a release of the forces within him pent up by the frustrations of the previous night at Valpena, and was steeling herself to meet it with fortitude. At any moment he would pounce, sweep her up into his arms and carry her into that equivocal bedroom. She must do her best to respond, but she was so tired and shocked by the events of the day that her own emotions seemed to have atrophied. She could only hope they would revive under Niccolo's kisses. What she needed was tenderness and petting, not his fiery demands, but that was something he would not give her.

When at length, finding the silence oppressive and puzzled by his lack of response, she raised her lids to look at him, anticipating meeting burning ardour in his gaze, she saw that his face was devoid of expression and his eyes were cold and hard as jet. She shivered, in spite of the warmth of the summer evening. Had she made an appalling mistake?

'D ... don't you want me?' she faltered.

'Want you?' Niccolo echoed. He laughed harshly. 'Not on your terms, *bianca rosa*. You made a charming gesture, but I do not appreciate sacrifices.' A gibing note crept into his voice. 'For that is what you are offering, *cara*, every inch of you proclaims it. Being a generous little girl, a grateful girl, anxious to pay your debts, you are prepared to immolate yourself upon the altar of my desire.' He got to his feet and walked to the window. With his back to her, he went on, 'I do not make bargains with my women, Lucy, they come to me gladly because they want to. Our need is mutual. I thought at Valpena ... but no matter, I have learned since that I was wrong.'

'Oh, Nicco, you're wrong now ...' she began, hurt and bewildered by this rejection when she had expected rapturous acceptance, but he cut her short.

'Do not perjure yourself, you made your real feelings only too plain by running away.' He swung round to face her, and his eyes were accusing. 'I left Valpena this morning believing you were pledged to me, but when I arrived in Syracuse I was met not by an eager *fidanzata* but with the news that you had fled without leaving a word of explanation. That came from Caterina, and she assured me you could not get away fast enough. Not very flattering, was it?'

'But, Nicco, I thought you would be relieved to find me gone. Oh, I see!' She looked at him contritely. 'By not marrying me you'll lose your inheritance, I'd forgotten that, but surely the Conte will understand you were not to blame for ... for ... my escape.'

'You have not escaped yet,' he said ominously.

All her doubts and fears returned with added force. Niccolo no longer desired her, for so she construed his rejection of her offer, but he did not want to offend the Conte who had so much to bestow.

'So that was why you were so anxious to save my life,' she cried bitterly. 'You stood to lose too much if I got away.'

'You are talking absolute nonsense,' he returned coolly. 'I do not accept bribes any more than I take unwilling women. I do not want Papa's wealth, I have enough for my own needs, and great wealth is a dangerous responsibility these days.' He grinned suddenly. 'But you, I was told, rendered his threats null by securing your testimonial. Caterina considered that the height of effrontery, but he would never have implemented them, he was bluffing you.'

'Charming family, aren't you?' Lucy said contemptuously, riled by this revelation of the way the Conte had manipulated her. 'For sheer low cunning you take some beating!'

Niccolo raised his brows. 'So you include me in that category? What has become of the gratitude that prompted your noble offer?'

'Oh, Nicco,' she was overwhelmed with remorse, 'I didn't mean I don't appreciate ...' she caught the mocking gleam in his eyes. 'You're laughing at me— and anyway you scorned it.'

'Oh no, *carissima*, never that. I know what it cost you to make it.' He put his head on one side, regarding her with the familiar sleepy sensuous look; he was his old teasing self again. 'Perhaps if when we reach Erice and you are rested you care to repeat it, I might have second thoughts.'

But it was no laughing matter to Lucy, and her heart swelled with indignation.

'You've a hope,' she said rudely. 'I don't cast pearls before swine.'

'How very apt! So now I am a swine?'

'Oh, dear, now I've provoked you again! Believe me, Nicco, I'm very, very grateful to you.'

She gazed at him appealingly, her eyes wide and earnest. He turned away from her to the window, absently rubbing the pane.

'You need not keep abasing yourself. I came after you as much for Caterina's sake as yours.'

'The Contessa?' she queried, astonished.

'Yes. In Papa's absence it was my duty to protect the family honour. Caterina could not be permitted to commit such a crime, which I am sure she would regret bitterly when it was all over.'

Lucy thought that was very unlikely, and doubted whether Niccolo believed it himself. But she supposed he felt he had to try to defend her. The Conte too would be shocked to discover his game with them had ended in such a tragedy ... or would he? He would probably consider a nondescript nannie no great loss in an over-populated world. She was considerably piqued to learn that Niccolo had not been motivated entirely by concern for her safety.

'I suppose the Santa Croce honour is sacrosant,' she said icily.

'It is,' Niccolo said proudly.

At that moment he was very much the Sicilian and Lucy realised the matter of family honour did indeed

mean a great deal to him, for though actually he was
of no blood kin to the Santa Croces, they belonged to
his class and clan. It awoke no responsive chord in her,
in fact it seemed outdated and a little absurd. To her
way of thinking Caterina di Santa Croce was no orna-
ment to any respectable family and did not deserve
defending.

'Well, I'm glad to know that my obligation to you is
less than I supposed,' she said with hauteur. 'But I've
no wish to increase it. I imagine it would be possible to
hire a car here to take me on to Palermo, so I need
trouble you no further.'

'Now you are being ridiculous. You are under my
protection from now on, and I am taking you to Erice.'

Lucy was about to tell him that she was nothing of
the sort, and she would go where she pleased, when she
remembered that Giuseppe might still be lurking in
the vicinity seeking an opportunity to carry out his
commission, and she said acidly:

'I suppose I must do as you say in case the Contessa's
henchman again puts the family honour in jeopardy.'

'Quite so,' he observed drily. He left the window and
came to sit down again in the chair opposite to her. He
offered her a cigarette, and when she refused, lit one
himself. He seemed more relaxed as if after having
cleared the air of misunderstandings, he was prepared
to be friendly.

'You are quite determined to return to England?' he
asked, rather to her surprise.

'After what has happened during the last two days
I shan't feel secure until I'm home again,' Lucy told
him. It was not only the menace of Giuseppe she was
thinking about. Where Niccolo was concerned she

could not trust herself; he was unpredictable, his attitude towards herself changing with each shift of mood. He had only to beckon and she would follow.

'Yes, your experience of my countrymen has been a little unfortunate,' he conceded, which Lucy thought was an understatement.

'I don't appreciate being the heroine of a melodrama,' she declared, 'or should I say, the victim?'

'*Poverina*,' he smiled kindly, 'Sicily can be rather strong meat for the unwary, and you are much too good-looking to be a nannie. Caterina was right there, Papa should have allowed her to send you back.'

In which case she would never have fallen in love with him, and thus saved herself much heartache, but she could not regret the experience; it would be something to look back upon all her life, a glowing patch of colour among the uniform grey.

'It would have saved you quite a bit of trouble if I'd gone,' she observed.

'Ah, do not say that. I will never regret our ... er ... moments together. I only wish I had got to know you better.'

The audacious glance which accompanied this sentence made his meaning clear, and she hastily changed the subject.

'These friends of yours at Erice ...'

'The Antonellis? You will find them much more congenial. They may restore your faith in my countrymen, though actually they are more Italian than true Sicilian. They originated in Calabria, which was my mother's country and where I too have an estate.'

'I'm sure they're delightful,' she said politely, 'but how are you going to explain me to them?'

'The simplest way would be to say you are my *fidanzata* and I wanted to introduce you to them before you left for England.'

'No, please, you mustn't tell them that,' Lucy declared earnestly. 'I can't consent to any more play-acting.' Already she had posed as his wife, been suspected of being his mistress, and had only just thrown off the role of his fiancée. She did not want to assume it again, even though it was fiction. 'We will tell them more or less the truth, that I had an accident on the way to the airport—after all, we nearly did—and you ... helped me. To make it more realistic I could wear a bandage.'

'Which would be another pretence,' he pointed out. '*Ecco*, I will tell your story, but we will leave out the bandage. I will say you were too badly shocked to proceed on your journey.'

'Yes, I've been exceedingly shocked in every sense,' she assured him feelingly. 'It won't matter very much what they think, as I'll soon be gone.'

A fact which gave her no comfort, for when she had left she would never see Niccolo again, and although that was the wise, the sensible course, it produced a feeling of desolation.

Niccolo blew a smoke ring towards the ceiling.

'Tell me about your home,' he bade her. 'You have brothers, sisters?'

She shook her head. 'No, there's only me. I live with my parents except when I'm away on a job. They're a very ordinary couple, and I'm very fond of them. My home is in Barford, it's a manufacturing town in Yorkshire, a very different place from here, a bit grim and dreary, but the hills aren't far away. Whenever I get a chance, I love walking on the moors.'

In her mind's eye she saw the grey town, under the usually grey sky, relieved by the long green slopes of the distant hills, which she could see from her bedroom window in their small suburban house. Very different from the colour, sunshine, blue sea ... and violence ... that was Sicily.

'You will look for another situation?'

'Of course, but ...' she smiled wanly, 'I'll not go abroad again, at least not for some time.'

'You gain satisfaction from tending other people's children?'

'Yes, I love children, that's why I trained to be a nannie.'

'It seems rather a bleak prospect to me, Lucy.' Niccolo moved in his chair, and stubbed out his cigarette. 'Perhaps you had better reconsider and marry me after all.'

She stared at him blankly. 'You're joking!'

'I am quite serious. I could at least provide you with material comfort.'

There could only be one reason for his persistence. He still needed a smoke-screen to conceal his relationship with Caterina, or perhaps he was afraid Lucy would talk and betray what the Contessa had tried to do to her and wanted to ensure her silence.

'I shall have to marry someone,' he went on, thereby supporting the first and least welcome of her suppositions. 'It will be expected of me.'

'I thought you were waiting for Carlotta,' she parried. 'As for myself, I've always earned my living and I shall continue to do so. Thank you for your offer of ... of comforts, but I don't want to be kept.'

'So I cannot persuade you?'

'You certainly can't.' He looked at her appealingly, and she burst out desperately: 'You know we were both coerced into that engagement, which neither of us wanted, you less than I did.' He made to interrupt her, but she hurried on: 'Don't try to spare my feelings by pretending otherwise. I understand yours exactly.'

'Do you indeed?' He gave her an odd glance.

'Yes. It was as much for your sake as mine that I decided to leave.'

'Do you dislike me so much?'

'Now *you* are being absurd, but oh, Nicco, what possible happiness could we find together?' she cried passionately. 'Our ways of life are totally different, and ... and you don't love me, and I ... I don't love you. Only love could bridge the differences between us, and there is none between you and me.' She turned her head away, as she denied her heart, fearing her eyes might betray her. He studied her in silence for some moments, her bent silver-gilt head, her white strained profile, then he sighed.

'Perhaps you are right, we do belong to different cultures. And I did rather lose my head, but I could have sworn we were *en rapport*.' He looked at her questioningly, but she gave no sign. 'You need fear no repetition. I will take care of you until you are on the plane to England, and then you can forget all that has happened here.' He flashed her his charming smile. 'Will that be all right?'

'Thank you,' she murmured faintly. 'You're very kind.'

He smiled sardonically.

'Kindness is not a national characteristic of ours, except towards children. But I will not destroy any more of your romantic illusions. You are dropping with fatigue. It would be a kindness to put you to bed ... your own bed, of course, but you will have to wait just a little longer. Shall we go?'

Seated once more in his car, Lucy noticed the new suitcase which Niccolo had put on the back seat behind her, and recalled that he had told her he had bought her some necessities.

'Did you get me some night things?' she asked as he slid in beside her and started the engine.

'Those and a few other trifles. You would not want to have to borrow from my friends.'

'That was very thoughtful of you, but I wish you hadn't had to bother.'

'My privilege,' he returned gallantly. He shot her a mischievous glance. 'I purchased for you *una camicia da notte*, a change of underwear and a few toilet articles.'

Lucy blushed. Circumstances seemed to be always forcing her into intimacies with Niccolo. Buying her underwear!

She said with constraint: 'You must let me pay you for it all. I've plenty of money.' She felt no scruples about taking the Contessa's lire. She owed her more than her salary for the fright she had given her.

'May I not make you a parting gift?' Niccolo asked softly. 'Please accept my small offerings, Lucy.'

'Well, thank you very much,' she said inadequately. Her indebtedness to him seemed to be mounting, and he refused payment of any sort. She would do her best to be gracious to these unknown friends since he wished to take her there, it was the only recompense she could offer.

Niccolo turned to the right and began to ascend a winding route up the mountain. As they went higher and higher the violet dusk began to fall. The flat plain fell away beneath them, the last light of the afterglow shining on the roofs of the houses, and turning the saltpans to the south into silver. The windmills looked like toys, until pinewoods obscured the view like a covering carpet. Lucy noticed with a shiver the sheer drops on either side of the road; her nerves were shaken by her recent experiences and she thought how fatally easy it would be to go over the edge to instant destruction. She glanced at Niccolo's dimly seen profile, and as if guessing her thought, he said cheerfully:

'Dramatic scenery, is it not? But have no qualms —I know this road well and I am not Giuseppe.'

He went on to tell her that a cable car went up and down making the ascent and descent quick and easy for tourist visitors, but he usually came by car.

'Erice is very old,' he continued as if seeking to distract her thoughts from the dangerous road. 'In Roman times it was linked with a shrine to Erican Venus maintained by priestesses whose sacral law bound them to bestow their favours upon all who asked for them. Most of their lovers expressed their gratitude appreciatively and some of them grew very rich. But alas, these revels ceased when the Romans went and the Normans built a castle on the ruins of the shrine. Venus surrendered to Mars, and the city of love became a fortress.'

'Would you have been among the votaries of Venus?' Lucy asked pertly.

'You mean the customers of the votaries. Probably, but you *mia piccola santa*, would appreciate a nunnery more than a temple. Tell me, do you get a kick out of being virtuous? It is usually the other way round.'

This was tending towards topics which she wanted to avoid, and she said hurriedly:

'I can't say I've ever been tempted.'

'Oh?' There was a wealth of meaning in that exclamation, and Lucy recalled how very nearly she had succumbed at Valpena, but now they had reached the top of the hill and were passing between the ancient walls of the mountain city and her attention was diverted to her surroundings. The car lights shone on clean stone-paved streets, with white stone borders and illuminated courtyards and quaint corners filled with flowers and greenery with here and there the grey bulk of medieval buildings. Niccolo drove into a quiet square and stopped before a yellow stone house. A few lines of light showed between the slats of the shutters, which were closed. Above them the stars were beginning to appear. It was very silent and peaceful and much cooler than on the plains they had left.

Niccolo said: 'I think I had better tell them you were in the Santa Croce employ to account for our acquaintanceship. I cannot treat you as a stranger, Lucy.'

'Tell them what you please, so long as you don't say I'm your fiancée,' Lucy returned, 'but you must keep your distance, Signor Martelli, Sicilian aristocrats look down on nannies.'

'This one thinks they are delightful,' Niccolo retorted, as he swung himself out of the car. 'Until they begin to sharpen their claws on me!'

He seemed to have recovered his usual lightheartedness, which had been in eclipse at Trapani. It must be the prospect of meeting his friends. He was whistling gaily, the familiar tune of *Santa Lucia* as he ran up the steps and knocked vigorously on the imposing front door with the brass knocker. If I were his nannie, Lucy thought, I should tell him not to make such a fiendish din!

The Antonellis welcomed them warmly. They were a charming family, Papa and Mama beaming with bonhomie, Mama taller than her husband but equally plump with a charming smile. Being of mainland Italian origin they were more exuberant than the Sicilians, and it transpired they had known Niccolo all his life. There were two daughters at home, aged fifteen and seventeen, the sons were away. The elder one, Maria, had a calm, beautiful face and a reserved manner. Later Lucy learned that she had a vocation and when she was eighteen would be accepted in a convent as a postulant. Beatrice, the younger one was lively and pert, she quite obviously had a crush on Niccolo.

Niccolo had phoned them before leaving Trapani to advise them of his arrival with Lucy, and they were full of sympathy for her 'accident'. She wondered wryly what they would have thought of the true story. They were acquainted with the Contessa and surely would have been deeply shocked. Niccolo told them she was leaving her employment because Carlotta was going to school. She hoped he would not invent too many falsehoods or she might make a slip; not that it mattered, when she would soon be gone.

After she had been offered refreshment, which she refused, Signora Antonelli insisted that Lucy must go to bed. Her wan looks substantiated her story. Beatrice

was deputed to conduct her to her room and make sure
she had all she wanted. The room she had been given
was small and comfortably furnished, with an old-
fashioned bedstead. Niccolo carried up her case and
deposited it at the door with a casual '*Buona notte.*'
Beatrice watched him walk away with a soulful expression, and as she joined Lucy in the bedroom gave a
deep sigh.

'*Comè meravigliosa* to be succoured by Niccolo!'
All the family spoke English, and the girls had had an
English governess. She looked at Lucy. 'And you only
a *bambiania*!'

She did not mean to be condescending, but naturally
she was surprised Niccolo had taken so much trouble
to assist a dependent. It was as well to be reminded of
her lowly position, Lucy thought, and she had the
satisfaction of knowing that if she had wished she could
have been presented as someone much more important.

'He is very kind,' she said non-committally.

'He is wonderful,' Beatrice enthused. 'He would
help anybody. You are tired, let me unpack for you.'

She opened Lucy's recently acquired case, and after
removing a layer of tissue paper, shook out a nightdress and negligee which Lucy saw to her horror were
not nylon but pure silk.

'How beautiful!' Beatrice caressed the filmy folds,
and gave Lucy a sidelong look. 'The care of little ones
must be very well paid.'

'I haven't much else to spend money on,' Lucy said
glibly. 'And having to wear plain things in the daytime,
I'm a bit extravagant about night wear.'

'And of course Nicco recommended the only exclusive shop,' Beatrice sighed. 'He has no idea of economy, that one.'

The Antonellises were not nearly as well off as the Santa Croces.

There were two sets of gossamer underwear, panties, bras and underslips, a toilet bag, and a brush and comb which Lucy saw with relief looked cheap and ordinary, but finally...

Lucy stared at the black dress which Beatrice was holding up and gazing at ecstatically. It too was of silk with a chiffon overlay, fashioned with a square neck and puffed sleeves. When did Niccolo imagine she was going to wear that?

'That will be *meravigliosa* for dinner tomorrow night,' Beatrice decided. But her brown eyes were curious as it was an extravagant purchase to make in an emergency.

'I couldn't resist it,' Lucy told her, inwardly fuming at Niccolo's indiscretion. 'A ... a sort of parting present to myself from Sicily. But by tomorrow night I shall have gone.'

'Oh, but you must stay until you are quite rested,' Beatrice declared. 'And I doubt if you will get a reservation tomorrow. It is too late to ask for one tonight and of course you will have lost the one you had—the planes are very full at this time of the year. Do put it on now, if you are not too tired. I would love to see how it looks on you.'

Lucy hesitated; she was longing to try on that glamorous garment, which Beatrice was not to know she was seeing for the first time. Somehow she must find a way to return it to Niccolo; she could not accept anything as expensive as it was, even as a parting present.

But meanwhile, there was no harm in trying it on. She had never possessed anything so elegant before.

Lucy slipped off her soiled white uniform and Beatrice lifted the black dress over her head and pulled up the zip. It fitted perfectly. Niccolo, Lucy reflected wryly, was very observant where women were concerned. He had gauged her measurements accurately. The soft folds clung to her supple figure and the sombre colour enhanced the fairness of her skin. She had never dared to expose it to the fierce rays of the Sicilian sun and it had retained its pearly whiteness.

'*Bella, bella!*' Beatrice cried, clapping her hands. 'Oh, how I wish I were a blonde, then Niccolo might look at me as he does at you.'

'I hadn't noticed he looked at me in any particular way,' Lucy said calmly, hoping she had not blushed. Beatrice must be very perceptive, for she had only been with the family for a short while before coming upstairs, and Niccolo had been occupied in exchanging greetings with their hosts. 'Signor Martelli is very fond of you all,' she added vaguely to placate the girl.

'He thinks I am still a child,' Beatrice complained disconsolately. 'But me, I am fifteen and a woman now.'

She drew herself up, thrusting out her chest which proclaimed the truth of her words. Latin girls mature young, and with her big brown eyes and sleek black hair, Beatrice was very attractive.

'I'm sure Ni ... Signor Martelli will have noticed that,' Lucy said reassuringly.

'Do you think so?' Beatrice brightened. 'Was the Contessa very horrid to you?'

The abrupt change of subject disconcerted Lucy.

'She decided I didn't suit,' she said carefully.

'No, you do not look like a children's nurse,' Beatrice declared. 'But nobody can get on with the Contessa, she has the temper of a fiend. The only person she is nice to is Nicco, but everyone loves Nicco.'

Lucy made no comment about that. She reached for the zip behind her, as there came a knock on the door.

'*Avanti*,' Beatrice called, and it opened to disclose Niccolo standing on the threshold.

'I came to enquire ...' he began, and stopped as he caught sight of Lucy. 'I thought you were going to bed.'

'So I am.' She was overcome with confusion; she had decided to return the dress and that he should have caught her trying it on was exceedingly embarrassing.

'She looks lovely, does she not?' Beatrice said wistfully. 'I told her she must wear it tomorrow night if she is still here, and you will stay too, please, Nicco?'

'Yes, I shall be staying,' he said absently, his eyes still fixed upon Lucy. 'That dress becomes you as I knew it would.'

'Were you with her when she bought it?' Beatrice asked.

He turned his head to look at her and recalled the situation.

'I took her to the shop, she was dazed, you understand, and needed ... support.' He spoke solemnly but there was a wicked glint in his eyes. 'Don't you think we both have excellent taste?'

'Do you mind?' Lucy intervened, fearing what he might say next. 'This is my room and I am about to go to bed.'

'*Scusi*,' Beatrice made for the door. 'I will run a bath for you, *signorina*. You take that dress off and then you come straight to it. The bathroom is next door.'

She ran out, leaving the door wide open behind her.

Lucy fumbled for the back zip and instantly Niccolo was beside her.

'Allow me.'

The zip slid down and the dress fell away, revealing her bare shoulders. From behind her, Niccolo's arms went around her, below her breasts, pressing her against him. He drew his mouth across her bared back, and kissed her below her ear.

'Nicco, for heaven's sake!' she gasped, helpless in his constricting hold. 'Beatrice ...'

'Is not here.' He laughed softly. 'I am claiming the price of the dress, so you need not hesitate to accept it.'

He kissed her again under her other ear, a long lingering pressure.

'*Vengo presto!*' Beatrice called. 'It is ready.'

Reluctantly Niccolo dropped his arms.

'Good night, *bianca rosa*, sleep well.'

He was gone. Lucy stepped out of the dress and mechanically picked it up. She laid it on the bed and reached for the negligee. As usual when Niccolo embraced her, her pulses were hammering. Beatrice called again and composing herself as well as she could, Lucy picked up the toilet bag and went into the bathroom. The tiled bathroom was full of the scent of the violet bath essence Beatrice had lavishly poured into the bath.

'May I stay and talk?' the younger girl asked, as Lucy slipped off her pegnoir.

'If you wish.'

She took off her underwear and stepped into the scented water. Beatrice seemed fascinated by her.

'You are lovely, lovely,' she declared. 'You have many *amanti* in England?'

'Oh, I've several boy-friends,' Lucy told her mendaciously, feeling it was expected of her.

'Boy-friend? But is not that the same thing? Me, I am not allowed boy-friends, my parents are old-fashioned. In due course I shall have a *fidanzato*.' She sighed. 'If only it could be Nicco!'

'Isn't he a bit old for you?' Lucy asked, soaping herself.

'*Non importa*, but I would not mind to be his mistress.'

'I'm sure you parents wouldn't approve of that,' Lucy said, reaching for a towel. There were several large fleecy ones warm from a heated rail.

'*Mamma mia*, they would throw a fit!' Beatrice giggled. 'But you, you are not shocked, *signorina*?'

'I'm past being shocked by anything,' Lucy told her as she got out of the bath, wondering if she should give Beatrice a lecture upon the dangers of promiscuity, but that was her parents' business, not hers.

Back in the bedroom, Beatrice reverently hung the black dress on a hanger while Lucy slipped into the high old-fashioned bed. She said goodnight and left her. The spots below Lucy's ears where Niccolo had kissed her seemed to be burning. Payment for the gown indeed! She decided that when she left Erice she would leave it behind her. It might fit Beatrice, they were much of a size. Beatrice was older than Carlotta and ripe for marriage. Perhaps Niccolo ... She fell asleep.

CHAPTER NINE

Lucy slept until midday. When she awoke she thought it was still early morning, for the light coming through the windows from which the shutters had been drawn back was subdued. She lay staring round the unfamiliar room as the events of the previous day came back to her. This was her last morning in Sicily. With luck she would be in England by nightfall. She ought to send a message to her parents to apprise them of her arrival, but they were not on the telephone. Perhaps she could send a wire.

The door opened and Beatrice peered round it.

'*Ecco*, you are awake at last.' She came into the room. 'I looked in earlier, but you were still sound asleep and Mamma said not to disturb you. You were tired out, *si*?'

Lucy sat up, pushing back her braided hair.

'What time is it?' she asked.

'Oh, past midday.'

'*What?*'

'There is no hurry. It is not a good day—there is a cloud over the mountain. It sometimes happens so. I will have your *colazione* brought up to you . . .'

'But Beatrice, I mean Signorina . . .'

'Please call me Bea, I would like you to do so.'

'Yes, thank you, but my reservation. I hoped to leave this afternoon.'

'But Lucia . . . I may call you that?' Beatrice sat down

on the bed, 'that is not possible. Niccolo has booked a reservation for you tomorrow at midday.'

'Oh dear, wasn't there anything sooner?'

Beatrice assured her there was not and that they would be delighted if she stayed. 'It is not kind of you to want to go so fast,' she reproached her.

'It isn't that—I felt I was being an imposition.'

'Oh no, no, you must not think that,' Beatrice protested. 'We love to have you and I want you to tell me all about England, and you will be here for dinner, to wear the beautiful dress.' She clasped her hands. 'Nicco stays too, so we shall have a lovely party tonight.'

The mention of Niccolo caused Lucy's pulse to flutter. She had been steeling herself for the final parting, but this was a reprieve. Had he by any chance engineered it? But that was wishful thinking; one way and another she had caused him a great deal of trouble, and he would be glad to be quit of her. It must be correct that he could not obtain a place for her on an earlier flight.

'Does Signor Martelli often stay here?' she asked, not daring to believe that he was staying for her sake.

'Whenever he is this way,' Beatrice told her. 'We always keep a bed made up for him.'

So he must come fairly frequently, and he had known Beatrice since she was a child. He would have noticed her blossoming womanhood, and her youth and freshness were a great contrast to the Contessa's mature charms. Niccolo had said he would have to marry someone and the daughter of his old friends would be very suitable in spite of the gap in years. Lucy was glad that she had refused to pose as his fiancée, which might have nipped this budding romance. At the same time her heart ached a little; she was so well aware she was not suitable and she had earned the Contessa's animosity, which she hoped Beatrice would be spared.

'Don't let me keep you from him,' she said.

'He is not here now, he has gone out with Papa,' Beatrice told her. 'But he will be here tonight. After you have eaten, we will go out, *si*?' She walked to the window. 'I think the mist is lifting.'

Lucy found her clothes had been laundered and by the time she had finished the meal brought up to her on a tray, only a few wisps of mist remained. Beatrice took her to look at the somewhat grim-looking church, with its massive bell tower built by the Aragonese in 1314. Inside she admired the statue of the Madonna and Child and the marble altarpiece.

When they came out the last of the mist had dispersed. Beatrice conducted her to an open space outside the town, from which the panorama surrounding the city could be seen, Trapani, the Aegadian Islands, and the high ground which lay between Erice and the Gulf of Castelamare. On the other side were ranges of mountains and in the far distance, the island of Pantelleria and the African coast.

'It is beautiful, *si*?' Beatrice said, 'but it is not friendly. I like the little places where there are many people. Maria now, she comes here to contemplate. Soon she will be shut away behind grey convent walls. Brr!' She shivered in the warm sunlight. 'That life is not for me.'

Lucy thought of the priestesses Niccolo had mentioned, whose duties had been the opposite of what Maria's would be, and his dig at her for being more suited to a nunnery. But he could not believe she was cold, not after the way she had responded to him; it had been prompted by pique because she had withdrawn from him. She felt a surge of regret that she had not taken what he had offered. Then she would not be leaving on the morrow and perhaps her love would in time have been reciprocated, and she would supersede the Contessa in his affections. But Caterina was a formidable obstacle, she had always been the barrier between them, and until she consented to let Niccolo go there could be no chance of happiness for his wife. How far jealousy would take her had been illustrated only too clearly by the events of the previous day. So long as Lucy remained in Sicily the Contessa's spite would pursue her and seek to drive a wedge between her and Niccolo, if not worse. It was possible those same events would finally alienate him from her, but he had tried to excuse her. Lucy had never been able to gauge what were his true feelings towards Caterina. He had implied it was all on her side, but his actions contradicted him. She could never forget how she had first seen him leaning in easy intimacy over the Contessa's couch.

She glanced at the young eager girl beside her. Should she give Beatrice a word of warning that if she became involved with Niccolo she would make an enemy of the Contessa? But she shrank from doing so. She might be wronging Niccolo, who had always denied he was intimate with Caterina, and if he had any sense he would take his young bride to Calabria out of the Santa Croce orbit. That he had never suggested such a course to herself supported her assumption that he had no genuine feeling for her. Beatrice was different, she belonged to his caste and country, but none of it was any affair of hers. She was going away and had no right to try to influence their destinies.

'Now you too are sad,' said Beatrice, watching Lucy's mobile features, which were more expressive than she knew. 'Do you think of a loved one far away?'

Lucy smiled wanly; her loved one was no further than the town behind them!

'I have no loved one, as you put it, I was reflecting upon the follies of mankind.'

'Yes, men are very foolish,' Beatrice took her literally. 'And I cannot believe that there is not one who adores you. You are like a princess in a fairy-tale, but perhaps that is it, the right prince has not yet come along to claim you.'

'Princes don't look at nannies,' Lucy returned, 'at least, not in the right way. Don't make up romances about me, I'm a very ordinary, down-to-earth person.'

'That I do not believe,' Beatrice declared. She linked her arm through that of the other girl. 'We are *simpatica*, are we not? I wish you were not going so far away.'

'Perhaps you'll come to England some time,' Lucy, suggested, as they started to walk away. 'Then we might meet.'

'Ah, *si, si,* Papa has spoken of it. Then you show me your country as I show you mine. You must leave me your address, *amica,* and I will write.'

That of the drab little house in Barford? Lucy smiled wryly; she could not see this colourful child in her environment, and probably when Beatrice came, if she came, she would have gone away to another job. But she did not mention that possibility, for if Beatrice did write she would be a link with Sicily ... and Niccolo, and she would not be entirely without news of him.

Even if they became engaged, she would like to know that he had some prospect of happiness which he could never find while Caterina had him in thrall.

Lucy decided that she must wear the black dress for dinner that night, for she could hardly appear in the white one which she had worn all afternoon, and it was for this eventuality that Niccolo had bought it. She could not plead lack of a gown since Beatrice had seen it, and would be sure to make some awkward remarks if she did not appear in it.

She brushed her hair until it shone and coiled it round her head. She wore no make-up beyond a touch of the lip stick which she carried in her handbag, and a dusting of powder which Beatrice provided. She was not allowed cosmetics, she said wistfully; her *mamma* said they were only for tarts.

But Lucy knew as soon as she came into the *salotto* that evening that she had made a mistake by wearing it. Signor and Signora Antonelli greeted her with polite enquiries—was she thoroughly rested, did she feel no ill effects from her 'accident'?—but their eyes were cold and their expressions critical. Though kindly people they had a position to uphold, for although Italy had officially abolished titles, they still abounded in Sicily and they wanted one for their child. Niccolo would presumably inherit one eventually and they had hopes of a match between them. They had given one daughter to the church, and could be excused if they had worldly aspirations for the other. This young woman whom Niccolo had foisted upon them was too pretty for her own good, and if she had been employed by the Contessa as a nannie, she was only a superior servant and her right place was in the kitchen, not the *salotto.* Yet he treated her as an equal and she had come down to dinner wearing what looked like a couture gown. No reason why a nannie should not buy one if she could afford it, but what would she want with one unless she had designs above her station? Young Niccolo could not take his eyes off her. They began to have doubts about the reason for her dismissal.

With her host and hostess withdrawing into disapproving silence, and Niccolo, after a perfunctory greeting, devoting all his attention to Beatrice, Lucy would have been isolated if Maria had not taken pity on her, for the incipient nun took her religion very seriously, and the church taught that all men ... and women ... were equal in God's sight if not in that of her parents. She asked questions about England and Lucy's impressions of the island, but took no real interest in Lucy's answers.

Lucy's heart swelled with indignation against Niccolo. He had insisted upon bringing her here, and given her the dress, which he should have known was totally unsuitable, she knew precisely what the Antonellis were thinking and he had not even the grace to give her his support. Perhaps he was avenging himself for her refusal to pose as his fiancée. He could retort that if she did not like her position she had only herself to blame, since he had offered her a better one. That she was not deceiving anyone gave her only poor satisfaction.

Niccolo was wearing a dinner jacket, his luggage had still been in his car when he dashed off after her. He looked sleek and elegant, but though he seemed anxious to show his indifference by flirting lightly with Beatrice, his gaze kept straying towards the girl in

black, as his host had noticed. Lucy resolutely kept her
head averted from him, though every nerve was conscious of his vivid personality. It was during the general
move when dinner was announced that he spoke to her.

'Why the icy disdain?'

'Work that out for yourself,' she retorted. 'My position is not enviable.'

'But . . .' They were swept apart.

At the table she was seated on her host's right hand,
with Maria beside her and Niccolo and Beatrice opposite to them.

Niccolo devoted himself to the Signora, who was next
to him, throwing an occasional teasing remark to
Beatrice. Signor Antonello unbent towards Lucy; like
all Italians he was susceptible towards a pretty woman
and after all, she would be leaving next day. The flower
arrangement in the middle of the table shielded him
from his wife's possible disapproval. He paid Lucy
several compliments and talked about England which
he said he hoped to visit in the near future. He knew
London, but of course he had not even heard of Barford. Somewhat pointed questions about her work in
the Santa Croce household Lucy successfully parried.
The food was good, and to her surprise Lucy enjoyed
her dinner, though she had to prevent her host from
refilling her glass. She knew what Marsala could do to
her.

The dinner hour was very late, as is common in Latin
countries, and when the meal was over, Lucy asked if
she might retire, as she had a journey on the morrow
and she was still fatigued. No one sought to detain her.
Niccolo came to the door with her, saying so all could
hear:

'You know your flight leaves tomorrow at midday, Miss Loring, and a seat has been reserved for you,' he held the door open for her and she passed through. 'I will arrange transport for you to Palermo...' He followed her and closed the door, keeping his hand on the handle. 'You look very lovely in that dress, *bianca rosa*, as I knew you would. Oh, *amore mia*, I cannot let you go!'

His dark liquid eyes met hers full of anguish, and Lucy felt colour flood her face, and dropped her lids over her eyes to conceal their instant response.

'I have to go, Nicco,' she said quietly. 'You know that.' She moved towards the stairs, and he followed her. Turning to face him, she added: 'You didn't have much consideration for me this evening, leaving me unsupported to face your friends' disapproval.'

'Did you want me to make love to you in front of the whole family?' he asked reproachfully, 'for if I had come to you, that is what I would have done.'

'Oh, really, Nicco!' She laughed a little forcedly.

'It is true. I would have claimed you as my *fidanzata*, and that you said I must not do.'

'No, there has been too much play-acting...'

'Play-acting! *Dio mio*, Lucy, you will drive me mad! Do you not understand, I cannot let you go because I love you.'

She paused, her foot on the lowest stair, and looked back at him. 'Is that true, Nicco, or is it the Marsala speaking?'

'You think I am drunk?' he said fiercely. 'Will you never believe that I am honest? From the first moment I saw you, you bewitched me. Since you are what you call a good girl, I would have married you, but no, you were frightened of the fiery passions of Sicily, so you run away. I saved you at risk of my life, and what is more important, my precious car,' he smiled, ruefully, 'all day yesterday I tried to behave as you would wish, not as I wanted to, but still you say you must go.'

Lucy gazed at him in bewildered amazement, wondering if she could believe her own ears. His face, within a few inches of her own as she stood above him on the stair, was quivering with emotion, the nostrils slightly flared, his eyes ablaze.

'You ... you love me?' she stammered.

'Must I say it again and yet again? But what are words!' His hands were on her waist, to pull her down to him.

'Nicco ... someone will come!'

'Let them!'

The *salotto* door rattled. 'Nicco!' Beatrice called.

Lucy wrenched herself free and went up two steps out of reach. She did not want Beatrice to find her in Nicco's arms. Instinctively she knew she would be hurt; if she had to be told it must be broken to her gently. Her own feelings were so chaotic she needed a little time to compose herself. A scene with Beatrice was more than she could face.

Beatrice had come into the hall, and Niccolo had turned to face her. She glanced from his flushed face to Lucy's embarrassed one with a slight frown, as she said:

'We want you to make up a four for cards, Nicco, if you have quite finished discussing Lucy's travel arrangements.'

'Yes, yes, of course,' Niccolo murmured distractedly. He glanced up at the girl standing above him, a slim

dark shape in the dim hall light, only her pale face and
shining hair fully illuminated. 'Goodnight, Lucy, I
will see you tomorrow.'

'Lucy?' Beatrice exclaimed. 'You use her first name?'

Niccolo had recovered his composure, and he grinned.
'Only in private,' he returned urbanely. 'One cannot
stand on ceremony with a girl who is wearing the dress
one . . . er . . . chose for her.'

'Then will you not choose one for me?' Beatrice
asked provocatively.

'Upon the first opportunity,' Niccolo promised her,
'but we are keeping Lucy from her bed.'

Before she could guess his intention, he went up the
few steps between them, and taking her face between
his hands deliberately kissed her full upon her lips.

'You certainly must choose a dress for me if that is
what comes of it,' Beatrice remarked.

'An old English custom,' Niccolo told her—with
more truth than he knew, for in Elizabethan times men
often 'bussed' girls, as they termed it. He went back
down the stairs and casually put his arm about Beatrice.
'I often kiss you.'

'Only when I was little,' Beatrice protested. 'But I
am big now and it is not the custom in Sicily, unless
you ask my permission.' She held up her face invit-
ingly.

'May I?' Niccolo asked perfunctorily. But he kissed
her cheek, not her lips.

'What goes on here?' Maria's cool tones fell like
snowflakes on a hot grid, as she came out of the *salotto*.

Beatrice giggled. 'Nicco is demonstrating old English
customs.'

Maria looked at them suspiciously and up at Lucy,

who, still palpitating from Niccolo's kiss, stood where he had left her, one hand clutching the banister, unable to tear herself away.

'Imported by our guest?' she asked icily; then recollecting that nuns should have no uncharitable thoughts, she went on: 'All in fun, I am sure, but Mamma and Papa want you both to make up a four at cards, and the Signorina Loring is going to bed.'

Lucy was recalled to her senses.

'Goodnight,' she called, and ran up the rest of the stairs.

While she undressed she went over what Niccolo had said. He had admitted that he loved her, said she had bewitched him from the first. He had tried to behave to win her confidence; she smiled tenderly at that —poor Niccolo, who it seemed believed his strong passions had frightened her. She had fled from him believing he did not want to marry her, and she had been quite wrong. He had followed her, risked a nasty accident for her sake, brought her to his friends for sanctuary and purchased an expensive wardrobe for her so that she would not be embarrassed by her destitute state. It was not his fault that he had not realised he had overdone it by the gift of the black dress. She smiled tenderly again as she hung it up; no lover could have done more for her, and Niccolo had declared he did love her. It had been the wrong time and in the wrong place, but he had said, tomorrow.

Tomorrow! Lucy lay in bed in a state of blissful anticipation. He had told her he could not bear to let her go. Well, she would not go. Tomorrow she would explain all her hesitations, confess how much he meant to her, and their engagement would become a reality instead of a manipulation of his stepfather's. She fell into a dreamless sleep murmuring his name.

Lucy awoke to bright sunshine. There was no cloud over Erice this morning, and she took it as a happy augury. Her dress had again been washed; she must remember to leave a handsome tip for the unknown laundress. She bathed and dressed while her heart sang a triumphant paean. Niccolo loved her, he had admitted it. If there had ever been anything between him and Caterina it was over, finished. But now she was ready to accept his assurances that there never had been. Why had she been so ready to think there was? Niccolo had to be polite to his benefactor's wife, and those languorous glances of his were what he bestowed on any woman under fifty. It was second nature to him.

She packed her case wondering where she would be that night, where Niccolo would take her. Not back to Syracuse, where the Contessa was now her open enemy. Perhaps to a hotel until they could be married. She would make amends for all her unjust doubts by trusting him entirely. Ironically they had his stepfather's blessing, for the Conte would still be anxious to hurry on their nuptials for his own reasons, particularly since they had been away together, though he would not know that the bond between them was not consummated love but their joint danger under the threat of violent death ... She hoped he would never learn the truth about that, for such knowledge would not improve the love-hate relationship between him and his wife.

She felt a qualm when she thought of Beatrice, for she liked the girl and she had been friendly, but she was sure all Beatrice felt for Niccolo was an adolescent crush; she had no expectation of anything more permanent. Neither of the two girls had any inkling of Beatrice's parents' ambitions for her.

Lucy came blithely down to breakfast, but to her disappointment, only the sisters were present. Signora Antonelli always breakfasted in her room, and her husband had gone out apparently with Signor Martelli.

'The vines again, I suppose,' Beatrice said resignedly. 'Perhaps they have developed a blight or something. But do not worry, Lucy, Nicco will be back in plenty of time to take you to the airport. He is most reliable.'

Lucy was not worried, and they would not be going to the airport. She would see him later and they would have all the summer day together.

But when Signor Antonelli returned, he was alone. He came into the breakfast room looking very grave and Lucy felt a premonition of disaster.

'I have ordered a hired car to take you to the airport,' he said to Lucy. 'Signor Martelli had to leave for Syracuse.'

Lucy stared at him blankly. Why on earth should Niccolo go back to Syracuse? After what the Contessa had tried to do, surely he must want to avoid her. It was Beatrice who demanded to know what had happened.

'A call came for him late last night when you had all retired,' Signor Antonelli told them. 'The Contessa had been trying to contact him all over the Island and finally she located him here. The Conte di Santa Croce has had a stroke, and he may not survive. Naturally Niccolo left at once.'

'If he dies Nicco will be the next Conte,' Beatrice said with satisfaction. Her father looked shocked.

'Hush, child, it is to be hoped he does not die,' he reproved her, 'but apparently his condition is very grave.' He absently poured himself a cup of coffee from the percolator. In spite of his reprimand, his thoughts were running in the same direction as his daughter's. He went on thoughtfully: 'The title is hereditary, and Nicco is not his son, but possibly he will assume it, if the money and estates have been left to him. His step-father always gave him to understand that in the absence of a son of his own, he was his heir, after making provision for Caterina and Carlotta, of course.'

He looked speculatively at Beatrice and there was an avaricious gleam in his eyes.

Lucy recalled that Niccolo had said he did not want this dangerous heritage, but that was when he thought he might have forfeited it. He might feel differently when it was actually within his grasp. He had gone, that was the devastating fact which caused her heart to plummet. Gone, before she had had a chance to tell him how much she loved him and that she would do anything he wished. Had he forgotten she would be leaving today? Probably, for her poor little affairs would have been obliterated by this family crisis. She could not delay her departure until he remembered her, for the Antonellises, with the exception of Beatrice, were anxious to see her gone, and there was no possible excuse she could offer for protracting her stay. All her bright anticipations had been wiped out by Signor Antonelli's news.

'When did he go?' Beatrice asked, depressed in her turn by the precipitate departure of her idol.

'At once, when he received the call, after midnight,' her father told her.

While Lucy had lain in bed fatuously dreaming about a glad tomorrow, a tomorrow which would never come.

Striving to make her voice sound casual, she enquired:

'I don't suppose he left any message for me?'

Signor Antonelli looked at her as if he had forgotten who she was, then recalling himself from his happy anticipations, he told her:

'*Così va bene*, he did.'

'Yes *signore*?' Lucy could not keep the eagerness out of her eyes.

He cleared his throat, hesitated, then said carefully:

'He asked me to wish you a pleasant journey and a happy reunion with your parents.' He avoided her anxious gaze.

So obviously Niccolo had become reconciled to the fact of her departure. After all, she had given no indication last night that she was ready to stay with him, rather the reverse. She had had no chance to make a proper response to his impassioned appeal, but if she had known what was going to happen, she would have made one even if it meant going to his room. She stared dismally at her plate. Nothing can recall a lost opportunity, and now she had lost him.

'*Ecco*, that was very civil of him,' Beatrice remarked. 'Did he leave one for me?'

Her father laughed. 'You will be seeing him again ere long, I do not doubt, but the *signorina* is going far away.'

Did he have to rub it in? Lucy thought ruefully, but she could see from his expression he was thinking the further the better.

The hired car came. Lucy was tempted to leave her case behind, its contents could only bring her bitter memories, but that would embarrass her hosts, who would feel they must try to send it after her. She thanked them politely for their kind hospitality, that was Signor Antonelli and the girls; the Signora had not yet appeared, but her husband promised to convey her thanks to her. A Sicilian girl she had not seen before was hovering in her bedroom, and Lucy gave her the gratuity which she obviously expected. She did not leave her address, and Beatrice had forgotten about it.

On reaching the airport Lucy collected her ticket, half hoping there would be a message from Niccolo, but the loudspeaker never called her name. She surmised that now he had to take over the Conte's affairs Niccolo had decided she was better out of the way, and if his stepfather died, Caterina would be free. That thought was predominant in her mind as she took her seat on the plane. Trained to administer the Conte's estates, beloved by Caterina, with an affection for her daughter, who was more fitted to step into his shoes than Niccolo? If a dispensation to marry was required, it would be procured. How could love for an English nannie weigh against all that? The message she had received was final, a pleasant journey, a reunion with her parents. As the aircraft was airborne she knew her summer in Sicily was over and she would never see Niccolo again.

Back in Erice, Signora Antonelli was brooding over a square envelope she held in her hand. Her husband had been wise to give it to her and not to the person

whose name was inscribed upon it. It was plain to her
that there had been something between Niccolo and the
English girl, and it was to be hoped her departure
would break it. Teresa Martelli had been her friend
and no one had rejoiced more than she did when she
had made her brilliant second match. If Niccolo was
to succeed his stepfather he needed a wife worthy of his
position, preferably Beatrice, of whom he had always
been fond. She owed it to Teresa's memory to protect
her son from a blonde foreign adventuress who was
seeking to divert him from his duty. Of course the
letter might be giving her her congé, but on the other
hand it might not. Yet being an honest woman, she
hesitated. When her husband came to tell her that the
guest had gone, she made up her mind. It was too late
now to deliver the missive, so it had better be destroyed.
There were matches and a candle on her bureau, as
the electricity sometimes failed. She lit one corner of
the envelope and held it over the china tray on her
dressing table. The paper flared, and before it sank to
ashes, two words stood out on its blackened surface,
'amore mia.' Yes, she had been quite right to burn it.

CHAPTER TEN

Upon her return to England, Lucy became very ill. Some bug she had picked up during her last few days in Sicily caused a high temperature, vomiting and other unpleasant symptoms.

The doctor who attended her was a local man whom she had known off and on for most of her life. The Carrs and the Lorings were friendly and Lucy had met Richard Carr at various local functions. For a while his name was linked with a Barford girl, Iris Mallory, who had been at school with Lucy. Then he left to train at a London hospital, Iris took up with another swain, and Lucy lost touch with them. Now Doctor Carr had taken up practice in Barford, sharing a surgery with three other doctors, and Lucy was on his list. She was some time recovering and during his visits they discovered a mutual fondness for good music. After her final visit to his surgery, when he pronounced her fit again, she being his last patient, he walked with her to the door to the street and electrified her by asking her to accompany him to a concert in the town.

Surprised, she stammered: 'I ... I thought doctors weren't supposed to hobnob with patients.'

'They aren't allowed to make passes at them, but you've been discharged and we're not in my surgery. Doctors are also human. You said you liked Chopin and Schumann, whose works are to figure in this concert, so why shouldn't we enjoy them together?'

That was the beginning. The concert was followed by another concert, then an evening at the ballet—Barford rated a number one tour by a well-known company—and then a walk on the hills one fine Sunday. They had found they were congenial companions with similar views on many subjects. Then Richard began to make significant remarks about a doctor needing a wife. Lucy regretted that; she liked him, she enjoyed his society, but she had no desire for a closer relationship. The memory of Niccolo was still too raw. Naturally she had heard nothing from Sicily, and she played with the idea of writing to Beatrice who might answer and tell her what had happened at Syracuse, but she decided she would be wiser not to attempt to contact her. Her sojourn in Sicily was something she had better try to forget, and correspondence with Beatrice would only reopen old wounds, especially if the girl became engaged to Niccolo. There was some news of Sicily in the papers. Etna had erupted and several rash tourists had been killed on their way to view the main crater, and some property had been destroyed, but it was not a major eruption, only a reminder of the sleeping giant's powers, and that it should be treated with respect. Vividly the account recalled to Lucy the night at Valpena and the firework display she had witnessed. Niccolo had asked if there were anything more beautiful than fire. His fire had scorched her heart, and though Richard Carr was seeking to pour balm upon it, he could never eradicate the scars.

Richard met her parents upon the occasions when he called at her home for her, and they heartily approved of him. They considered their daughter would make an excellent doctor's wife. She had a strong sense of responsibility, a knowledge of childish ailments, and in spite of her romantic appearance, a streak of practicality. She was better educated than they had been, and could hold her own at social gatherings. They would be thankful to have her settled nearby instead of going off to some strange foreign place in pursuit of her calling. She had not been quite the same since she returned from Sicily and though she had said nothing, they were sure something unpleasant had occurred there. She would not promise that she would not go abroad again. They did not know that she was seeking forgetfulness and thought she was more likely to find it in some interesting foreign country.

One job her agency offered her was the care of the infant daughters of some dignitary in Saudi Arabia, and Lucy had teased them by pretending to consider it.

'I rather fancy myself as another Anna in *The King and I*,' she told them.

'But that was in Victorian times,' her father protested, 'and Saudi Arabia is a dreadful place for an Englishwoman, with all sorts of restrictions.'

'You might end up in a sheik's harem,' her mother hinted darkly.

'I don't think they have them nowadays—and the salary's colossal.'

But she turned the job down. Her father urged her to take her time about procuring another post, for she still looked frail, and he wanted her to stay at home until she had regained her full strength ... or became engaged to Dr Carr, though he did not mention the latter possibility.

Lucy began to wonder if she was playing fair by going out with Richard if she had no intention of marrying him, when he might find someone more forthcoming. But she was beginning to rely upon his companionship, and would miss it very much if she ceased to see him. She knew she could do very much worse than marry him; she was not cut out for spinsterhood. Niccolo had roused vague yearnings that Richard could appease, and tending other people's children could become frustrating when she wanted a family of her own. She could never experience again the wild rapture she had felt in Niccolo's arms, she did not want to. He had almost destroyed her. Richard did not excite her, but she could depend upon him. He was a brown-haired, blue-eyed young man with the clean athletic wholesomeness of the best English type. He confided to her that he was shy of modern girls, who were so self-assertive and eager to proclaim their independence.

'A doctor's wife has to put the needs of others before developing her own ego,' he told her drily. 'She has to be nearly as dedicated as he is.'

'There must be plenty of serious-minded girls around,' Lucy said, 'but like most men you want something decorative, and that sort are usually spoilt.'

'But you're not spoilt, and you're the most decorative person I've met,' he returned. 'You've chosen a career which demands unselfishness, but wouldn't you like to have a family of your own?'

But Lucy was not ready to commit herself and she put him off with a flippant reply, but she did begin to consider him seriously.

It was several months since she had returned from Sicily. Summer had faded into autumn. One afternoon

Richard drove her out on to the moors and leaving the car they wandered among the dying heather, which still showed purple and the red and yellow bilberry plants already clothed in their autumn livery. They found a sheltered spot under an escarpment of rock and sat down to rest surveying the ridges and peaks around them. A curlew uttered its plaintive cry and up in the blue sky, a hawk hovered.

'He let you down, didn't he?' Richard asked suddenly.

Lucy stared at him, astonished. 'What do you mean?'

'My dear, I'm not blind, and I've got to know you fairly well. Sometimes there's a lost look in your eyes, at others you go off into a dream, and when I speak to you you look round in eager anticipation which turns to disappointment when you realise it's only me.'

Lucy laughed to hide her discomfiture.

'Good gracious, Dr Carr, I'd no idea you'd put me under your microscope—and I'm sure your imagination has been working full time!'

'Don't fence with me,' he rebuked her. 'You must know by now that I think a lot of you, but I'm fully aware there's someone else who means more to you than I ever could.'

'There's no one else,' Lucy said steadily, 'not now. It was when I was in Sicily, and he was ... is ... devastatingly attractive.' Her eyes became dreamy. 'A sort of Italian Adonis, but he was related to a Sicilian count and I was ... just a nannie.' She moved uncomfortably. 'The episode had a melodramatic ending, and I ... I'd rather not talk about it.'

Richard muttered something about damned dagoes under his breath.

'Oh, he was prepared to do the honourable thing,' Lucy cried quickly. 'He offered to marry me, but his family ... er ... intervened ... so I ... came home.'

'I should think so!' Richard exclaimed. 'He couldn't have been serious about marriage. You were crazy, dear, to take a situation abroad and expose yourself to such advances.'

'Lots of girls do, and I wanted to see something of the world.'

'But your colouring is an incitement to Latin males, who haven't a good reputation.'

She returned lightly. 'So because of my colouring I must be condemned to stay in England?'

'Your excursion into the romantic Mediterranean didn't do you much good,' he pointed out. 'You came back looking like a ghost. But I could suggest a much more, I hope, congenial position for you.'

There was no mistaking the look in his eyes and Lucy drew a long breath.

'No,' she whispered. 'Please, no!'

Richard sighed. 'It's too soon, I suppose. But you can't waste all your young life regretting a dream. Lucy, I mayn't look like an Adonis and I haven't any Latin fire, but I can offer you a steady affection and keep you in comfort.'

She noticed he did not mention love, and she recalled Iris Mallory, but Richard had not then been in a position to marry.

'Are you also a reject?' she asked bluntly.

He reddened. 'You mean Iris? That was only a boy and girl affair and she wouldn't wait. It's all past history.'

Lucy laid her hand on his arm sympathetically.

'But it hurt, didn't it? God, don't I know how it hurts!'

Richard put his hand over hers and said huskily:

'You could make me forget her, Lucy and perhaps I could comfort you.'

But Iris had been some years ago, Niccolò only a few months.

'I may forget in time,' she told him, 'but I can't expect you to wait indefinitely.'

'I'm a patient man, Lucy.'

She had a sudden vision of Niccolo's dark, vivid face. He was not a man who would be willing to wait for what he desired. She still ached for him and it was hardly fair to expect Richard to fill the void he had left, and she doubted if he could.

'You might wait in vain,' she warned him.

'I'll take my chance of that, you're worth waiting for.'

'I'm not,' she cried wildly. 'If you knew . . .'

He frowned slightly. 'Lucy, I don't want to know what passed between you and him, but I'm sure he was the one to blame.'

'No, I was as bad.' Then as she met his anxious gaze, 'I don't mean I slept with him, it didn't go that far.' But it so nearly had.

'It wouldn't make any difference to me if you had,' Richard assured her, but she sensed he was relieved. 'Forget him, Lucy, as I made myself forget Iris. We must both look forward and not back.'

She sighed. 'Richard, I want to get back to work, that will help me most, but if, after six months, you're still of the same mind, I may be ready to accept your offer. But perhaps Iris will come back?'

'She won't, she married someone else.'

'She may not stay married,' Lucy remarked, thinking of the Contessa who might be a widow by now and
after a year's mourning, again a wife. Not that Iris's
husband was likely to die, but no marriage in England
nowadays could guarantee permanency.

'I wouldn't want to bank on that,' Richard returned,
and laughed, but his laughter held no merriment, and
Lucy knew he still loved the other girl as she did
Niccolo.

To her parents' dismay, Lucy held to her resolve to
seek another job. She was filled with restlessness and
lack of an occupation fretted her. She might take a
temporary post while she sorted herself out and made
up her mind about Richard.

It was raining when she went to see her agent; a grey
curtain obscured the hills, the town itself wore that
dismal aspect common to English provincial cities in
the wet. Lucy ascended in the lift to the third floor of a
tall concrete building, but even the acres of glass windows did not give sufficient light in the dreary murk to
obviate the need for supplementary electric light. A
smart young receptionist in a brown suit greeted her.

'Mrs Ashley will not be long, if you'll take a seat.'
Then she recognised Lucy. 'Oh, you're the nannie who
went out to Sicily—did you like it there?'

Lucy envisaged the brilliant sunshine and the
luxuriant vegetation of the Golden Ribbon in contrast
with her present surroundings, they seemed like an
exotic dream.

'It was very beautiful and I enjoyed the sun, but I'm
glad to be back.

The receptionist returned to her desk and Lucy sat
down. Mrs Ashley was not only her agent, but a friend,

as her mother had worked with her before her marriage. There was one other occupant of the room, a
young woman sitting huddled in a corner as if she
were cold. There was something familiar about her, but
Lucy could not place her. Like herself she was wearing
a raincoat with a hood, which obscured her face, but
whereas Lucy's coat was white, hers was dark brown.
Voices sounded from Mrs Ashley's office, though the
words were not audible. One was low and deep, the
other Mrs Ashley's precise tones, and once Lucy
thought she detected a child's treble. Not applicants
for a job, presumably, but possible clients, though they
usually made their requests by phone and the prospec-
tive employees were sent to be interviewed.

The door flew open, and Lucy rubbed her eyes, believing she was having an hallucination. There was
Mrs Ashley, mature, but with a good figure and grey
hair beautifully styled, and the couple she was showing out were Niccolo and Carlotta.

Mrs Ashley was saying: 'As I told you, I don't know
if she is still disengaged, and if she is, I doubt if she will
want to go to Sicily again, but I'll contact you ...' She
broke off, for Carlotta's sharp eyes had identified Lucy
under her disguising hood.

'It is Mees!' she cried, 'my *bambinaia*! You said we
would find her in England, Zio Nicco, and here she is
come to meet us!'

She ran up to Lucy and threw her arms about her
neck.

The woman in the dark raincoat stood up, pushing
back her hood, and Lucy saw it was Giulia. She returned Carlotta's embrace, feeling completely bewildered.

'It seems your quest is ended,' Mrs Ashley remarked. 'Miss Loring,' she was always formal before strangers, 'this gentleman is visiting England and requires a nannie to take charge of his ward, that little girl, and he asked for you because you looked after her before, but I told him you didn't want to go to Sicily again, as you didn't ... er ... find the conditions quite what you expected.'

Lucy heard little of this explanation. Over Carlotta's head, her eyes were fixed upon Niccolo. He was wearing a suede car coat, the collar turned up against the autumn chill, his black head rising proudly above it, but there was a light in his black eyes which she could not mistake.

'*Dio mio*,' he exclaimed, 'Lucy at last!' Then as he recollected that they were not alone, his face became expressionless and his lashes veiled his eyes as he turned to Mrs Ashley.

'As you say, madam, my quest is ended. I need not take up any more of your time. This lady is the one I wish to engage.' He took out his notecase. 'How much do I owe you?'

'Half a minute,' Lucy interposed, recovering her wits. 'I don't know what all this is about, or how you come to be here.'

Surely the Contessa could not have sent him to re-employ her?

'I will explain everything in a more suitable place,' Niccolo told her smoothly. 'Sufficient for the moment, you are coming back to Italy with us as soon as you have packed your cases. Carlotta and I ... and poor Giulia too ... have had enough of this rain soaked country.'

'That's rather precipitate,' Mrs Ashley said stiffly. 'I understand Miss Loring doesn't wish to go. She found her former position unsuitable.'

'It was not,' Niccolo agreed. 'I am about to offer her a very much better one.'

'Then of course she will expect a bigger salary.'

Niccolo smiled. 'She may ask what she pleases. All my worldly goods are at her disposal.'

Mrs Ashley looked taken aback, wondering if the man was mad. She glanced at her assistant and saw she was gaping at Niccolo with the expression most women wore when they met him. She was completely hooked. Carlotta cried in her shrill treble:

'My *bambinaia* isn't going to be my *bambinaia* any more. She is going to be my Zia Lucia. We are all going to live in Calabria, and Zio has horses for me to ride, and I can gallop where I please, not like that horrid school. There will be no nasty Franco to watch me all the time, and I can paddle and learn to swim.'

Mrs Ashley put her hand to her head. 'Lucy,' she forgot to be formal, 'can you make head or tail of that rigmarole?—because I can't!'

She looked from Lucy's radiant face to the man's impervious one. So this was the explanation of the girl's sudden return from a job which was to have lasted several years with a blank look in her eyes and a story about having been considered too young. This imperious young man was no doubt the cause of her dismissal, but now he had arrived in England demanding her re-engagement. From Lucy's expression she would follow him to the ends of the earth if he requested it, but did she know what she was doing?

The ou er door opened and a severe-looking lady in

the full regalia of a nannie's uniform stalked in. She glanced in surprise at the group of people who were not sitting correctly on the chairs provided for them, and the manageress of the establishment, who was usually only accessible through her receptionist, looking slightly flustered.

'I had an appointment at eleven o'clock,' she said frigidly.

'Oh yes, Miss Green.' Mrs Ashley indicated her office. 'Come this way. Sandra, attend to your duties.' The receptionist jumped. 'Lucy,' her voice sank, 'don't do anything without consulting your parents.'

'We will go and see them now,' Niccolo decided, having overheard her.

'Yes ... well,' Mrs Ashley waved her hands helplessly. Then assuming her professional manner she turned to Niccolo with a mischievous gleam in her eyes. 'If you are requiring a really competent children's nurse, sir, the lady in my office is at liberty.'

Niccolo returned her look with a wicked glint in his. 'Thank you, madam, but I prefer the one I have got.' He turned away from her. 'Come along, all of you— Lucy, Carlotta, Giulia—we are impeding Madam's business.'

He shepherded them out, followed by Sandra's languishing gaze.

They went down in the lift, Carlotta clutching Lucy's hand and Niccolo reassuring Giulia, who was not used to elevators and was scared. They stepped out into the drizzle and walked a few paces to where the big car was parked, a hired one for Niccolo's journey north. He put Giulia and Carlotta into the back seat, and Lucy into the front one, saying as he did so:

'I had to bring Giulia to look after Carlotta. The poor infant has had a rough time and I hoped a trip to England might distract her.' He walked round and got into the seat beside her. 'Now direct me to your home,' he commanded.

'Before we start, I'd like to know what you're proposing I should do,' Lucy enquired, feeling it was time he gave her an explanation. 'From what you said you appear to have become Carlotta's guardian, and do you intend I should return to Sicily to look after her?' She looked at him searchingly, for she was hoping his intentions were more personal.

'Not to Sicily,' he told her. 'I am living in Calabria now, Valpena was destroyed by Etna's last eruption.'

'Oh, I am sorry. Was anybody hurt?'

'Not physically. Beppo and Paolina are in Italy, but I had a sentimental regard for that place.'

Carlotta drummed on the back of his seat.

'Zio, why do we not go? This place is ugly!'

'Infant, do not be so impatient.' He started the car. 'Which way, Lucy?'

Mechanically she started to direct him. She had no clear recollection of what he had said to Mrs Ashley, she had been too overthrown by the unexpected sight of him, but it would appear he was living in Calabria and wanted her to care for Carlotta who inexplicably had become his charge.

'How are the Conte and Contessa?' she asked in a low voice.

'Later—I cannot talk before the child. You understand?'

'I don't understand why you want to see my parents.'

'To ask their permission of course.'

'I make my own decisions about accepting situations.'

'I prefer to do things the proper way. Will your father be at home?'

'Yes, he's on holiday, and he won't go out as it's so wet.'

'So my luck is in for once!'

Lucy glanced at him nervously. She was beginning to guess what was in his mind. She saw that he looked older than when she had seen him last. Some of his ebullient lightheartedness had vanished, and the set of his mouth was grim. Whatever had happened in Syracuse had left its mark. Niccolo's insistence on seeing her father implied that he was still thinking of marrying her, and the thought took her breath away. But did he fully realise her humble origins? He would do when he saw the Lorings' unpretentious little house, so different from the imposing Villa di Santa Croce and the Antonellis' mansion at Erice. Her parents were homely people, she was not ashamed of them, but Niccolo might have a shock. She told him:

'I'm glad you're coming to my home, and I'm delighted you're going to meet my father. You will see then what my background is. If it ... isn't what you expected, I shall understand, and if after seeing it you change your mind ... about taking me back to Italy, I'll also understand. I love my parents and nothing could persuade me to drop them, so take a good look at them and the house, before you do ... anything rash.'

'Sometimes, *mia cara*, you do talk the most utter rubbish,' was Niccolo's bland reply.

The little house in a row with its diminutive strip of front garden surrounded by a privet hedge, its windows, one a bay downstairs and two sash ones above, all discreetly veiled in nylon muslin, looked bright and cared for in spite of the murky day. Mrs Loring waged an unending battle against dirt and smuts and her husband repainted the woodwork every three years.

'What a nice little place!' Carlotta exclaimed as they drew up outside the front door. 'It is like a house for dolls!'

They left Giulia in the car and walked up the short path to the front door. The brass knocker and letter box gleamed with polish and the edge of the one step that gave access to it was whitened along its edge, as were the stone ledges outside the bay. Northern women are very houseproud and never stint on elbow grease. Lucy opened the door with her key and ushered them inside, then a few steps down a narrow passage and in at the sitting room door. The room had a fitted carpet, bright patterned curtains and mock leather-covered settee and chairs. Compared with the *salotto* at the villa it was like a rabbit hutch. She bent down to switch on the electric fire which filled the grate. Then straightening herself, she looked Niccolo full in the face as she said defiantly:

'This is my home.'

His sweeping glance had taken in every detail, the few pictures, Constable prints, the beige satin-striped wallpaper, the television set and cheap bookcase filled with paperbacks.

'It is charming,' he said.

'It isn't, it's pokey, cheap, vulgar...'

He put a hand on her arm.

'Why so heated, *bianca rosa*? I never imagined you lived in a palace. There is nothing here to offend good taste, and it has a happy atmosphere.'

Somewhat mollified, Lucy took off her raincoat.

'Let me take yours, and do sit down.'

She carried the garments into the diminutive hall and hung them up. When she returned Niccolo was sprawled on the settee and Carlotta kneeling by the fire. They looked quite at home. Lucy was about to call her mother, when Mrs Loring came into the room. She had been cooking and wore a nylon overall, and there was a streak of flour on her nose. She was plumper and shorter than her daughter, but she had the same air of fragile prettiness, and the same lovely eyes. She stared in astonishment at the handsome aristocratic-looking man and the bonny child. Niccolo got to his feet as Lucy introduced him.

'This is Signor Martelli from Sicily, and his ... er ... niece. He's come to see me about another job.'

'Oh, don't say you're going out there again!' Mrs Loring exclaimed. 'Beg pardon, sir, but she came back half dead from there and we've only just got her well again.'

Niccolo swung round to look at Lucy.

'You have been ill?'

'Oh, it wasn't anything much.'

'Nothing much! Temperature a hundred and four, vomiting every hour, and thin as a rake. It must be a most unhealthy place!'

'Yes, I am afraid it was rather unhealthy for her,' Niccolo agreed. 'But it is Italy this time, *signora*.'

He was looking at Lucy with such tender concern that she felt completely unstrung.

'It's all the same,' Mrs Loring declared, 'I don't think she should go. I'll get her dad to speak to you.'

'It is her dad I have come to see,' Niccolo said gravely.

Carlotta had turned her attention to Mrs Loring's knitting bag and was pulling out needles, skeins of wool and the half-finished sweater it contained. Catching sight of the wreckage, Lucy cried:

'Oh, darling, you mustn't do that!' and glanced anxiously at her mother, but Mrs Loring did not scold.

'The kiddie's bored stiff,' she said comfortably. 'Come with me, sugar, and I'll find you some lemonade and a chocolate biscuit. What's your name, lovey?'

'Carlotta,' the child said, going to her.

'There now, isn't that a pretty name? Come along with me. I'll send Dad in to you,' she said over her shoulder to the other two.

Lucy replaced the scattered articles. She could not bring herself to look at Niccolo, who seemed to be enjoying himself.

'Your mother has a way with children,' he remarked. 'I have never known Carlotta go to a stranger before.'

Then David Loring, thin, stooped, with his daughter's regular features and silver-gilt hair, shambled in. He fixed mild blue eyes upon the visitor.

'You wanted to see me, sir?'

'I have a request to make of you. Lucy, go and join your mother, this is men's talk.'

Lucy was so surprised at his sharp tone that she meekly went.

'You won't go to those nasty foreign parts again?' Mrs Loring demanded. Carlotta was ravaging a packet of chocolate biscuits with detriment to her fingers and mouth. Lucy went to fetch a face cloth without replying.

Presently her father called to them from the sitting room.

'Mother, Lucy, come here!' He sounded dazed.

Niccolo was standing in the middle of the room, a wicked grin on his face as they came in. He walked up to Mrs Loring and kissed her cheek. *Mia suocera,* he said. Only Lucy knew it meant mother-in-law. He turned towards Lucy and bowed mockingly. 'My adored one, I have your father's permission to pay you my addresses. I offer you my hand, my heart, my estate in Calabria and joint guardianship of this repulsive child.' He indicated Carlotta, still smeared with chocolate. 'Don't you dare to refuse!'

'Oh, Nicco!' Lucy went into his arms oblivious of spectators. 'Yes, yes, and again yes. Oh, I can't believe this is true!'

Niccolo insisted that they must all have lunch at his hotel to celebrate the engagement. While her parents were changing, and Carlotta was temporarily absent in the bathroom under Mrs Loring's supervision, he told Lucy briefly that the Conte was dead. After lingering for several weeks, another stroke had finished him. There was no time for more, as Lucy needed to renovate her own appearance. She had a leather jacket with a fur collar which would be more appropriate for a hotel lunch than her utility raincoat.

They ate in the public dining room, but without Giulia. As many of the staff were Italians she felt quite at home in the kitchen. Then at Niccolo's suggestion, the two elders agreed to take Carlotta to the cinema, assuming correctly that the lovers wanted to be alone. Since there was no privacy in the hotel, they dropped the picturegoers at the local Odeon and went back to the terrace house. There Niccolo told Lucy that upon his return to Syracuse that morning he had found absolute chaos. The Contessa seemed stunned, Carlotta was weeping and wailing, the servants at a loss. The Conte's collapse had thrown them all into confusion. He had been the mainstay of the household, directing and commanding; the Villa was like a ship without a captain and not even a second in command, until Niccolo arrived. By the time he had restored some sort of order, he realised that Lucy's plane would have gone, but he was not much concerned because she would have received his message and would understand. At which point Lucy stared at him blankly. How had he expected her to interpret that brief farewell as reassuring?

With the Conte helpless Niccolo had had to take control of his many activities. After his death there was even more to do. He had willed his estate to Carlotta to be held in trust for her and her children, after making provision for his wife and a behest to Niccolo with guardianship of the child.

'Which I think I shall have earned by the time she is of age,' he remarked drily. 'That is where you will come in, *amore mia*. I shall need your help to manage her.'

'But the Contessa?'

'Has elected to retreat into a convent. Papa's stroke was caused by one of their quarrels. It seems Giuseppe confessed to him what he had been engaged to do, fearing Caterina's wrath at his failure. Papa was furious at such a breach of hospitality. Caterina was overwhelmed with remorse—she has always been emotional to the point of being unbalanced, and she is also a devout Catholic. Blaming herself for Papa's death, she decided to do penance by renouncing the world.'

'Will she go through with it?' Lucy asked, unable to see the Contessa as a nun.

'I am sure she will, she does not do things by halves. After a few years she will be made a Mother Superior in recognition of the immense dowry she will bring with her.' He smiled cynically. 'I pity the unfortunate women in her charge.'

Then had come the destruction of Valpena, which he deeply regretted. He had been telephoning the house daily to know if there were any letter from herself.

'I asked you to write to me there as I could not come to you,' he said reproachfully, 'but you never did.'

Lucy told him she had received no letter from him; all she had had was Signor Antonelli's verbal message, which had indicated that all was over between them.

'The old ...' Niccolo used a rude word. 'I know he hoped I would marry Beatrice, but I never gave any indication that I was serious about her. I went to see them, hoping Bea might know your address, but she said you had forgotten to leave it. She was very sweet, she said she wanted to meet you again when we were married, and you were the luckiest girl in the world to have won my love. A sentiment which I hope you will confirm.' He gave her a mischievous look.

'Oh, I do, not many nannies are fortunate enough to acquire an estate in Italy.'

Lucy was sitting in one of the armchairs, hands demurely folded in her lap, while Niccolo lounged on the settee. Her composed face gave little indication of the exultation she was feeling. Niccolo had come to find her, he loved her, and the Contessa was immured in a nunnery.

'I said for winning my love, do not pretend to be mercenary. Or are you looking so prim and proper because I have not inherited Papa's fortune after all?'

'I couldn't care less, but I'm still confused. You came to England to engage a nannie for Carlotta?'

'When you did not write, I feared you had repudiated me. But I wanted confirmation from your own lips. I remembered Caterina must have had correspondence with the agency who recommended you, and I found the address among her papers. I was told upon contacting them that it was not correct to divulge employees' private addresses and that all business must be done through the agency. So I brought Carlotta to England thinking the change might benefit her, and went along to beard that grey-haired dragon on the pretext of re-engaging you. Oh, my love, I was full of trepidation, for I feared, having had no word, that you had banished Sicily and me from your thoughts, for which I could not blame you after your experiences there, and I should discover I had been superseded.'

'You nearly were.' Lucy could not resist the opportunity to tease him, who so often had teased her. 'As I didn't receive your note, I thought you were through with me, so I was contemplating marrying a most estimable young doctor.'

'Were you indeed?' He sat up abruptly, his black brows drawn together and his eyes smouldering with savage jealousy. 'Did you want to endanger his life? You are mine, Lucy, and no other man shall touch you.'

Lucy thrilled to the passion in his voice, though she was intimidated. What was she taking on with this dangerous man who looked capable of sticking a stiletto into poor Richard's back? She said hurriedly:

'Nicco, I thought I'd lost you and that you might be going to marry the Contessa.'

'*Dio mio!* I would as soon take a cobra to my bed. But she was Papa's wife. I though I had explained about her long ago. Did you ever believe it was otherwise?'

Lucy decided she had better hold her tongue about that. Her doubts had been born of jealousy which is an integral part of love. At last she was convinced they were groundless.

Niccolo was watching her downcast face and when he spoke again, his manner had changed completely and was quiet, almost humble.

'Forget what I said just now, it was the Sicilian part of me speaking, and you always did excite the beast in me.' He smiled ruefully. '*Carissima*, do not permit me to overrule your good sense with my impetuosity. If you have any reservations about the life I am offering to you, if in your heart you are secretly afraid of me and the passion which I cannot always control, then I will say no more. If you would prefer to remain in this damp, dark land,' he glanced disparagingly out of the window! Barford had not been kind to him weatherwise, 'which perhaps is more suited to your cool temperament than Italy's harsh sunlight, and if you would rather marry your worthy doctor, then say so now, and I will go away and cease to trouble you. For if you decide to come with me, there will be no going back, no compromise. I want all or nothing.'

She glanced in surprise at his still face. This aspect of him was quite unexpected. He was not looking at her, his eyes were fixed on the privet hedge beyond the window. He had turned pale and his mouth was set in a hard line, as if he were exercising immense control.

'Do you really mean that?' she asked.

'Your happiness is more to me than my own fulfilment,' he said gravely. 'Consider all the pros and cons and do what will be best for you. I will not attempt to persuade you either way.'

Lucy rose from her chair and went to kneel beside him, looking up at him with all her heart in her eyes.

'Nicco, I don't need to consider. There is no happiness for me outside your arms,' she declared earnestly. 'But I'm glad you said what you did, because I know you really love me.'

He turned his head and as her shining eyes met the flame in his, he pulled her up on to his knees. But his kiss was tender, his hold gentle. From different countries and diverse backgrounds destiny had welded them together with a great love that transcended all barriers. With her head on his shoulder, Lucy murmured:

'Take me back to Italy soon, darling, where perhaps the sun is shining.'

'Ah, yes, the sun.' He glanced at the greyness outside. 'Light of my life, with you beside me, our life will be sunshine evermore.'

'Amen to that,' Lucy said, and kissed him.

FREE Harlequin romance catalogue

A complete listing of all the titles currently available.

Harlequin Reader Service

IN U.S.A.:
MPO Box 707, Niagara Falls, N.Y. 14302

IN CANADA:
649 Ontario St., Stratford, Ontario N5A 6W2

Please send me my FREE Harlequin
Reader Service Catalogue.

Name _____

Address _____

City _____

State/Prov. _____ Zip/Postal _____

00356426100